Please return/renew this item by the
last date shown to avoid a charge.
Books may also be renewed by phone
and Internet. May not be renewed if
required by another reader.

BARNET
LONDON BOROUGH
www.libraries.barnet.gov.uk

K124

30131 04718609 0

LONDON BOROUGH OF BARNET

DOCTOR · WHO

Ghosts of India

DOCTOR · WHO

Ghosts
of
India

MARK MORRIS

BBC
BOOKS

2 4 6 8 10 9 7 5 3 1

Published in 2008 by BBC Books, an imprint of Ebury Publishing.
Ebury Publishing is a division of the Random House Group Ltd.

© Mark Morris, 2008

Mark Morris has asserted his right to be identified as the author of this Work
in accordance with the Copyright, Design and Patents Act 1988.

Doctor Who is a BBC Wales production for BBC One
Executive Producers: Russell T Davies and Julie Gardner
Series Producer: Phil Collinson

Original series broadcast on BBC Television. Format © BBC 1963.
'Doctor Who', 'TARDIS' and the Doctor Who logo are trademarks of the
British Broadcasting Corporation and are used under licence.

The Random House Group Ltd Reg. No. 954009.
Addresses for companies within the Random House Group can be found at
www.randomhouse.co.uk.

A CIP catalogue record for this book is available from the British Library.

ISBN 978 1 846 07559 9

The Random House Group Limited supports the Forest Stewardship
Council (FSC), the leading international forest certification organisation.
All our titles that are printed on Greenpeace approved FSC certified
paper carry the FSC logo. Our paper procurement policy can be found
at www.rbooks.co.uk/environment

Series Consultant: Justin Richards
Project Editor: Steve Tribe
Cover design by Lee Binding © BBC 2008

Typeset in Albertina and Deviant Strain
Printed and bound in Germany by GGP Media GmbH

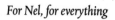

For Nel, for everything

Ranjit made his way cautiously through the densely packed neem trees and the green-blossomed champale. He was trying to make as little noise as possible, because he didn't want the monkeys to hear him.

He didn't like the monkeys. Sometimes they pelted him with fruit – rotten mangoes or poisonous berries. When that happened, Ranjit would throw stones, and the monkeys would scatter. He was afraid, though, that one day they might realise he wasn't so tough, and that although they were smaller than him, they were stronger, faster and more numerous.

In spite of the monkeys (not to mention the snakes, and the jackals that he sometimes heard baying out on the plain), Ranjit still preferred sleeping in the old temple to sleeping at the camp. The camp was full of sick people, crying women and hungry babies. It was a place of misery and despair, and he went there for three reasons only: to get food, to see Miss Adelaide, and to find out whether his Uncle Mahmoud had turned up.

In his heart of hearts, Ranjit didn't think he would ever see his Uncle Mahmoud again. Since his parents had died of cholera six years earlier, when he was five, Uncle Mahmoud had been his guardian. Ranjit knew his uncle was not the sort of man who would abandon him, which could only mean that something terrible had happened.

Terrible things were happening all over India just now. Every day more people were being killed in the violence that was sweeping the country. Calcutta was a war zone, which was why Ranjit could not go back to the house he had shared with his uncle. Thousands had already fled their homes, and no one seemed to know when it would all end. Some people seemed to think things would settle down once the English had gone home. But others claimed this would only make things worse, that without the English to govern the country, India would descend into civil war.

All Ranjit knew was that he was tired and needed to sleep. Slipping through the trees and the long grass, he came at last to the temple. It was a small temple in the Dravida style, with a squat porch supported by pillars. The tower was constructed of progressively smaller storeys of pavilions, and gave the impression of different-sized squares stacked in order, the largest at the bottom, the smallest at the top. Though the stonework had been elaborately carved, the building itself was long abandoned. It was festooned with vines, which were slowly forcing their way between the ancient, crumbling stones. Birds and insects had made their homes in the temple's nooks and crannies, and of course the monkeys used it as a playground. It wasn't much, therefore, but it was shelter. Plus it was quiet – if you ignored the rustling of beetles and cockroaches, and the distant cries of the owls.

It was stiflingly hot tonight. And the vast dark sky was full of strange, swirling colours – greens and purples and oranges. But at least the heat seemed to have driven the monkeys away. They were probably sleeping, conserving their energy. Ranjit didn't dare hope that they might actually have found a new home elsewhere.

He was walking across the clearing when he noticed the light in the sky. It hung above the temple, yellow as a firefly. At first Ranjit thought it *was* a firefly, even though he knew immediately that there was something odd about it. He craned his neck. How high up was it? A hundred feet? A thousand? A million?

Then he blinked. Was it his imagination or was the light getting bigger? A few seconds ago he hadn't been able to see the corona around it, but now he could. It looked like a great fiery mane.

He stared at the light for a few more seconds. Yes! It

was getting bigger! It was as if a hole was opening in the night sky, behind which a brilliant light was blazing.

Ranjit swallowed. Could he hear a soft roaring or was that the blood rushing through his head? He didn't know, but what he *couldn't* hear was the chirrup of insects in the undergrowth. Eerily, all the night-sounds he was used to had ceased. It was as if every living creature had suddenly become aware of the descending light and had stopped to look up at it.

All at once Ranjit felt very scared and alone. Something was happening. Something bad. The light was as big as a dinner plate now, its glow touching the top of the tower, turning it from black to gold.

Thirty seconds later, and Ranjit had to shield his eyes against its glare. Another thirty, and he had to *close* his eyes and slap his hands over his ears as the soft roar of the thing's descent rose to a thin scream, and then to an unbearable shriek.

The ground started to shake, as if about to split apart. Ranjit felt his bones shaking too, and curled up on the ground like a caterpillar, trying to block it all out. But it was no use. The light and the hideous shrieking were overwhelming. They poured into his body like water into an empty bottle, and he blacked out.

How long he remained unconscious he had no idea. When he came to it was dark, and the insects were back, trilling softly in the night.

He sat up, feeling weak and sick. His ears throbbed,

and his eyes were sore, but already the discomfort was fading. He looked up at the sky, and saw blackness studded with the white glints of stars. He blinked the soreness from his eyes, rose shakily to his feet, then turned and faced the temple.

Instantly he realised that the light had not gone, after all. Instead it had been swallowed by the temple. It was now streaming from the open porch and the cracks in the weathered stonework, pulsing bright, dim, bright again, like a glowing heart.

For a few seconds Ranjit stared, wondering what to do. He was apprehensive, but no longer frightened. Now that the light had fallen to earth, it was not shrieking, nor blazing like angry fire. In fact, there was something almost comforting about it, something inviting.

He found himself walking towards it, as if in a trance. He passed between the pillars of the temple, into the porch, and felt himself embraced by its radiance. Ahead was the antechamber, and beyond that the central shrine. Could he see something in the shrine, a dark shape, blurred by the dazzling illumination around it? As if dragged by invisible wires, he walked through the antechamber and into the shrine itself.

For an instant the light blazed brighter than ever, and the shape in the centre seemed to shimmer. Then the light settled into a soft, pulsing glow, and Ranjit saw clearly what it had been concealing.

Sitting cross-legged upon a golden throne was a vast figure cloaked in a tiger skin. The figure had three eyes, and on its head it wore the moon like a crown. Four arms jutted from the wide shoulders, two of which were at rest, hands folded in its lap, and two of which rose behind it, swaying slightly, like cobras preparing to strike. The figure's chest was bare, but around its neck coiled a serpent and a garland of human skulls. The figure looked down at Ranjit, impassive and serene.

Ranjit recognised the figure instantly. This was Shiva, the Lord of Sleep, the Fathomless Abyss. Shiva the Destroyer; Shiva the Howling of Storms; Shiva the Lord of Songs and Tears.

He began to shake with fear. He was unworthy to look upon the face of the Divine. He was committing a terrible trespass by being here.

He bowed his head and thought about asking for forgiveness, but his mouth was as dry as a desert and the words would not come.

In the end, utterly terrified and certain that he would be struck down at any moment, Ranjit turned and ran.

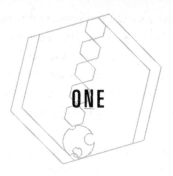

ONE

'Where now?' the Doctor said. He was like a kid at a funfair, trying to decide which ride to go on next. He stood poised, waggling his fingers, his face glowing green in the light from the TARDIS console.

Donna thought he looked like a string bean in a blue suit. A string bean with trainers and sticky-out hair.

'Dunno about you,' she said, 'but I could do with a breather.'

'A breather!' he said, aghast.

'Yeah, we're not all Martians, you know. Us humans need a little sit down and a nice cup of tea every so often.' All at once her eyes widened. 'You know what I'd *really* like?'

'Astonish me.'

'A curry.'

'A curry?'

'Yeah, I could murder a curry. I'm starving.'

The Doctor looked at her as if she was a prize pupil who had handed in a sub-standard piece of work. Then inspiration struck him, and he was off again, bouncing round the console, slapping and poking and twiddling things.

'Curry, curry, curry,' he muttered. 'If I can just… yep, there we go.' The grinding bellow of the TARDIS's engines started up and the Doctor straightened with a grin.

'Donna,' he said, 'prepare yourself for a taste sensation.'

In a narrow alley between two tenement blocks, dust began to swirl. The trumpeting groan of ancient engines rose out of nowhere, and as they built to a crescendo the faded outline of an old blue London police box began to solidify. No one saw the box arrive except for a famished yellow cat, which ran for its life. For a few seconds the box stood, immobile and impossible, dust settling around it. Then the door flew open and the Doctor sprang out, still in his blue suit and trainers, and now also wearing a red plastic sun visor on a piece of black elastic.

'Come on, Donna,' he shouted. 'You were the one who couldn't wait to stuff your face.'

'And you were the one who said I should dress for a

hot climate,' she retorted, emerging from the TARDIS in a flowery long-sleeved sundress, sandals and a wide-brimmed hat. She looked around. 'Where are we?'

'Calcutta,' he said, '1937. Brilliant city, full of bustle and colour. Still ruled by the British Raj, but it's the heart of India. Centre of education, science, culture, politics—'

'What's that smell?'

She was wrinkling her nose. The Doctor sniffed the air. 'That,' he said, 'is the scent of burning cow dung. *Bellisimo*. Come on.'

He strode off, Donna hurrying to catch up. She looked around at the shabby tenements with their peeling shutters and corrugated iron roofs. The ground was hard-packed earth. Flies buzzed around her head.

'Not exactly salubrious round here,' she said.

'Well, we don't want to be ostentatious. Don't want to frighten the goats.'

He grinned and she smiled back, linking her arm with his.

'So where you taking me?'

'Select little eatery. Belongs to an old mate of mine – Kam Bajaj. Helped him out once with an infestation of Jakra worms.'

'Wouldn't have thought pest control was your kind of thing,' Donna said.

The Doctor shot her one of his sidelong, raised-eyebrow looks. 'Jakra worms are from the Briss

Constellation. They're eight-foot-long carnivores. Imagine a Great White Shark sticking out of a hairy wind sock and you've pretty much got it. Anyway, old Kam said any time I fancied a free dinner…'

'Oh, charming,' said Donna. 'Cheap date, am I?'

'That's one advantage, yeah,' the Doctor said, smirking, 'but the food is out of this world. Macher jhol that melts in your mouth, beguni to die for, kati roll, phuchka. And the puddings… *caramba!* Rasagolla, sandesh, mishti doi…' He kissed his fingers like a chef.

'Chicken korma and a poppadom'll do me,' Donna said.

'I'll pretend I didn't hear that,' he replied.

They walked for twenty minutes, the Doctor leading them through a labyrinth of streets without once hesitating. Gradually the streets widened as they moved away from the poorer areas of the city, but even the change of surroundings didn't help Donna shake off a feeling of unease, a sense that something was not right.

The Doctor didn't seem to notice the shuttered shops and burned-out buildings; the debris scattered on the ground; the rats crawling around the stinking piles of uncollected rubbish; the gangs of young men who glared at them in baleful silence as they strode by. He kept up a constant jabber about Calcuttan life, one second talking about the August monsoons, the next about how he was once voted man of the match at the Calcuttan Polo Club. As they passed yet another group of silent men, some of whom brandished staffs or simply thick branches stripped of leaves, the Doctor raised a hand and called, 'Hello there!'

None of the men answered. One spat on the ground close to the Doctor's feet.

'Probably just shy,' the Doctor muttered as Donna took him by the arm and led him away.

'Blimey, for the biggest genius in the universe you can be incredibly thick sometimes,' she said.

'Oi!' he protested, then asked her more reasonably, 'What do you mean?'

'Just look around you. Even a mere earthling can tell that something's about to kick off here. You can virtually smell the testosterone in the air.'

The Doctor's eyes darted around. 'I suppose the atmosphere *is* a bit tense,' he admitted.

'Maybe we ought to head back to the TARDIS,' she said, 'settle for the Taj Mahal on Chiswick High Road.'

'Kam's place is only a couple of minutes from here. It's a lot closer than the TARDIS.'

Two minutes later they were standing outside Kam's place, looking up at it in dismay. It had been gutted by fire, the interior nothing more than a burnt-out hollow. Face grim, the Doctor placed his hand on a door frame that was now just so much charcoal.

'No residual heat,' he said. 'This happened a while ago.'

'Two weeks,' said a cracked voice to their left.

Donna looked down. An old man was squatting on his haunches in the shaded doorway of the building next door. He wore nothing but a turban and a pair of loose white cotton trousers. His skin was lined and leathery, and an unkempt grey beard covered the lower half of his face.

The Doctor darted across and squatted beside him. 'What happened?' he asked softly.

The old man shrugged. 'When men fight,' he said, 'their judgement becomes clouded. They bombard their enemies with stones and kerosene bombs and beat them with clubs. But if they cannot find their enemies, they simply destroy whatever is close by. They claim they fight for a just cause, but when the madness takes them they don't care who they hurt.'

'Yeah,' the Doctor murmured, 'I know the type. But what about the people who lived here? Kamalnayan Bajaj and his family?'

'They are gone.'

The Doctor's eyes widened. 'You don't mean…?'

The old man shook his head. 'No, no, they are alive and well. But they have fled Calcutta. I don't think they will return.'

'Not to this address anyway,' said the Doctor ruefully. 'But this can't be right. I know for a fact that Kam was here in 1941. I came for Navratri. I brought fireworks.'

'What's Navratri?' Donna asked.

'Hindu festival. Lots of dancing.' Thoughtfully he said, 'So either someone's mucking about with time or…' He turned back to the old man. 'What year is this?'

'1947,' the old man said.

'*Forty*-seven!' the Doctor exclaimed, and jumped to his feet. 'Well, that explains it.'

'Does it?' said Donna.

'Course it does. Think of your history.'

'Believe it or not, I wasn't born in 1947.'

'Not your *personal* history,' said the Doctor. '*Earth* history. Didn't they teach you *anything* at school?'

Donna gave him a blank look. 'I only liked home economics.'

The Doctor made an exasperated sound. 'Remind me to buy you a set of encyclopaedias for your next birthday.'

'Only if you remind *me* to punch you in the face,' Donna said.

The Doctor carried on as if she hadn't spoken, talking rapidly, almost in bullet points. 'Last year there was a famine in India. The people got desperate and angry. When the British Raj did nothing to help, the population rioted. Now the Brits are about to give India home rule, but instead of solving the problem it's only making things worse. Different religions are fighting amongst themselves about how to divide up the pie, and Calcutta is at the centre of it. At this moment it's one of the most volatile places on Earth. Thousands have been killed, many more made homeless. It's a massive human tragedy, and I've landed us slap-bang in the middle.'

He looked so anguished that Donna felt compelled to say, 'Well, nobody's perfect.'

He smiled sheepishly. 'The Taj Mahal on Chiswick High Road, you say?'

She nodded. 'There's a pay and display across the road, if you need somewhere to park.'

They said goodbye to the clearly puzzled old man and headed off down the street. It was still hot, and flies were still buzzing around their heads, but the cloudless sky had deepened, and the shadows were lengthening.

As the sun crept towards the horizon, more and more men were gathering in the streets. Almost all of them silently watched the Doctor and Donna pass by, their expressions ranging from bemusement to hostility.

'Just look confident,' muttered the Doctor. 'Usually works for me.'

'Don't worry, Doctor,' Donna said. 'Once you've been to a few West Ham/Millwall games, there's nothing much that can frighten you.'

They were walking down a quiet street, past a pile of straw and steaming dung, when they heard gunshots from somewhere ahead of them.

'Although in my time,' Donna said, 'people don't

usually shoot each other at the football. What shall we do?'

The Doctor halted and half-raised a hand. 'We could always stand here for a minute and hope it'll go away.'

The gunshots grew louder – and were now accompanied by the din of an approaching crowd.

'Any more bright ideas, Einstein?'

The Doctor pointed at the pile of straw and dung. 'Well, we could always hide in there.'

Donna gave him an incredulous look. 'I think I'd rather get a bullet through the head than cover myself in—'

'Shift!' yelled the Doctor, grabbing her hand.

The panicked cries of the crowd had suddenly become much louder. Donna turned to see that soldiers on horseback had appeared at the end of the street, and were driving a rampaging mob before them.

A mob that was heading straight for her and the Doctor!

'Where is that dratted Gopal?'

Dr Edward Morgan consulted his fob watch with a frown, then dropped it back into the pocket of his waistcoat. He looked tired, Adelaide thought, and with good reason. He worked such long hours at the camp that he barely allowed himself time to sleep. He could easily have settled for a cushy practice in the 'White Town', treating overfed English diplomats with the gout, or old ladies with the vapours. Instead, despite many of his fellow countrymen scoffing at him for wasting his medical skills on 'coolies', he had decided to ply his trade on the front line.

Adelaide had been so inspired by his commitment that she had openly defied her father, Sir Edgar Campbell, to help him. Sir Edgar continued to assert that tending to the ailments of Indians was 'a most unsuitable position for an Englishwoman', but at least he was fair-minded enough to allow his daughter to make her own decisions. The work was arduous and the rewards minimal, but Adelaide had the satisfaction of knowing that she was trying to make a difference.

'He'll be here, Edward,' she said. 'Gopal is reliable and dedicated.'

Edward used a crumpled handkerchief to wipe a sheen of sweat from his forehead. He was unshaven and his white doctor's coat was stained and dusty. He was in his late twenties, only five years older than Adelaide herself, but just now he looked closer to forty.

'I know he is,' he said, his irritation fading. 'I do hope nothing has happened to him.'

'Well… my tonga-wallah did tell me that there has been trouble in the north of the city again today,' Adelaide said. 'I believe Major Daker and his men are attempting to restore order. It could be that the streets are simply difficult to negotiate.'

'Yes, I'm sure that's what it is,' Edward said wearily,

and swayed a little on his feet. Adelaide, who had just arrived at the camp for the night shift, reached out to steady him. Her touch made him blink in surprise, and the look he gave her caused her to blush. To cover her embarrassment, she looked around the medical tent with its two cramped rows of beds and asked, 'Has it been a difficult day?'

Edward smiled without humour. 'No more than usual. We've had another fifty people in today, most suffering from malnutrition.' He wafted his hand in a gesture that somehow carried an air of defeat about it. 'The fact is, Adelaide, we simply don't have the resources to cope. I feel so helpless, having to stand by and watch children starve in front of my eyes… but what can you do?'

Again, Adelaide felt an urge to put a hand on her colleague's shoulder, but this time she resisted.

'You're doing your best, Edward,' she said. 'It's all anyone can reasonably expect.'

He shrugged and looked around the tent once again. Despite the best efforts of the overburdened medical staff, it was a squalid place. The patients slept beneath unwashed sheets, with swarms of flies hovering above them and cockroaches scuttling across the floor. The interior of the tent smelled of sickness and sweat and, even with the flaps pinned back, it was as hot as an oven during the day and barely cooler at night.

The tent was one of three, situated side by side on

a slight rise at the north end of the camp. The tents housed the most seriously afflicted of the refugees, who, over the past six months, had been arriving here in their hundreds, on this flat, dusty area of scrubland two miles outside Calcutta.

'How many deaths today?' Adelaide asked bluntly.

Edward sighed. 'Fifteen.'

She nodded stoically. 'Anything else to report?'

'We had another one brought in.'

She knew immediately what he meant and her fists tightened. 'The same as the others?'

Edward nodded wearily. 'She was a young girl, perhaps eighteen or nineteen. Two men brought her, bound like an animal. They didn't know who she was, and she was in no fit state to tell them. She has the same protrusions on her face and body as the others. The men say she was like a rabid dog, attacking people in the street. They told Narhari they believed the girl was possessed by demons.

'She had bitten one of the men on the hand. I treated the wound and tried to place him in quarantine, but he refused to stay. I only hope she hasn't passed the infection on to him.'

'We still don't know that it *is* an infection,' Adelaide said.

'And we don't know that it isn't either,' replied Edward, 'apart from the fact that none of us has yet been taken ill.'

She was silent for a moment, then she asked, 'Can I see the girl?'

'She isn't a pretty sight, I'm afraid.'

'All the same…'

Edward led her out of the tent and towards the one at the far end of the row. The sun had slipped below the horizon now and the sky was a riot of reds and purples, which would soon deepen to black. Out on the plain, the hundreds of people who had fled the fierce in-fighting between different factions of their countrymen were huddled in shelters made of wood and blankets and corrugated iron. The area was dotted with the flickering lights of fires, around which the recently homeless huddled for comfort and to cook what little food they had. Here and there scrawny goats, bleating piteously, were tethered to posts. Conversation among the people was soft and sombre. There was very little laughter, even from the children.

Edward held the flap of the third tent aside for Adelaide and she walked in. The interior of the tent had been divided in half, the front half partitioned from the back by several lengths of grubby muslin. They each donned a surgical mask, and then Edward led Adelaide through the flimsy partition. She braced herself. She was frightened of these particular patients, but she wouldn't avoid them. If she wanted to do her job properly, she couldn't afford to be selective.

There were twelve beds here, ten of which were

occupied. It was unusual for even a single bed to be standing empty, but this area had been designated an isolation zone. All ten patients had arrived in the past week, all suffering from the same mysterious symptoms.

The newest arrival, the girl, was in the fifth bed along on the left. Adelaide approached, dry-mouthed, even though she knew that the patient would be tethered and sedated.

Sure enough, the girl's hands and feet were bound by strips of strong cloth to the rough wooden bed-frame. She was sleeping but restive, her eyes rolling beneath their lids, her lips drawing back from white teeth as she snarled and muttered. She was small and slim, and Adelaide could tell that she had been pretty once. Her finely boned face was the colour of caramel, her hair like black silk. She wore a simple white sari, which was torn and stained with dirt, and her bare feet were lacerated with wounds that had been washed and disinfected.

As ever, it was the sight of the strange protrusions which horrified Adelaide. This girl had one on her forehead and one on her neck. They were black-purple lumps, which had pulled the flesh around them out of shape. From experience, Adelaide knew that the lumps would grow and multiply until the patient died. It had happened to three patients already, and two more were currently close to death. When the first sufferers had arrived a week ago, Edward and his colleagues had thought they were witnessing the start of a new strain of bubonic plague. But the limited tests they had been able to carry out seemed to belie that theory. So far they had failed to pinpoint any infection – which didn't necessarily mean there wasn't one.

'Does she have the pale eyes?' Adelaide asked, leaning over the girl. In all the cases so far, the victim's eyes had become paler as the illness progressed, as if the pigment was draining out of them. It was eerie, watching a person's eyes change from brown to the insipid yellow of weak tea.

'Not yet,' said Edward – and at that moment, as if to prove the fact, the girl's eyes opened wide.

They may not have been yellow, but they were bloodshot and utterly crazed. The girl glared at Adelaide, and then lunged for her so violently that the restraints around her right wrist simply snapped. As Adelaide jumped back, the girl's teeth clacked together, closing on empty air. Edward rushed forward to grab the patient's flailing arm, but her momentary surge of energy was over, and already she was slumping back, her eyes drifting closed.

'That shouldn't have happened,' Edward said, retying her wrist. 'I gave her enough sedative to knock out an elephant.' He looked up at Adelaide. 'Are you all right?'

Adelaide was already composing herself. 'I'm fine.'

She hesitated a moment, then stepped back towards the bed. 'Poor thing. I wish we could find out what's causing this.'

Edward said firmly, 'I still maintain that it's a chemical poison of some kind, perhaps similar to the effects of atom bomb radiation.'

A shiver passed through Adelaide. The American atom bomb attacks on the Japanese cities of Hiroshima and Nagasaki had occurred just two years previously, and had sent shock waves across the world.

'But if a bomb had gone off nearby, we would have heard of it surely?'

'It needn't have been a bomb,' said Edward. 'It could be something in the water.'

'Something introduced deliberately, you mean?'

He shrugged. 'It's possible.'

'Some of the staff here believe that the illness is something to do with the strange lights seen in the sky a week ago,' she said.

Edward snorted. 'Superstitious nonsense.'

She looked at him. Her eyes above the mask gave nothing away. 'I'm sure you're right, Edward,' she said evenly.

The Doctor yanked on Donna's hand. 'Come on!' he yelled. 'What are you doing? Pacing yourself?'

Donna stopped just long enough to raise a sandalled foot. 'It's not easy running in these things, y'know.'

'Well, why did you wear 'em then?' he shouted.

'Because we were *supposed* to be going for a quiet meal. You didn't tell me I'd need combat gear.'

The mob was gaining on them. From the quick glimpse she'd taken after the Doctor had grabbed her hand, Donna had been reminded of stampeding cattle, all wild eyes and mindless, headlong flight. But these 'cattle' were being driven not by cowboys but by British soldiers on horseback, wearing sand-coloured uniforms. At their head, barking orders and occasionally firing his revolver into the air, was a red-faced major with a bristling moustache and a peaked cap.

It was her own fault really, Donna thought. She supposed she should have known better. *Wherever* she went with the Doctor she usually ended up running away from something. He was the sort of man who could find danger in a boxful of kittens.

She was doing her best to put one foot in front of the other as fast as she could, but it wasn't easy; her sandals were in constant danger of flying off. The Doctor was virtually pulling her arm out of its socket as he urged her to run faster, but it was all right for him. He had a snazzy alien metabolism – *and* he was wearing trainers!

Eventually the inevitable happened – she slipped. As her feet went in opposite directions, she lost her grip on the Doctor's hand. She managed to stay on her feet, but next thing she knew someone was barging into the back of her. Even as she was swept up in the crowd and carried along as if by a fast-flowing river, she heard the Doctor shouting her name.

'Donna!' the Doctor yelled again as the fleeing crowd caught up with them. He tried to make his way through the throng towards her, but the people were too tightly packed, and too panicked by the galloping horses and the crack of gunfire to allow him access. For a few seconds longer he glimpsed Donna's distinctive red hair, and then it became submerged in the mêlée. The Doctor decided the best thing for now was to go with the flow and pick up the pieces later.

He was being carried along by the crowd – which reminded him of the time he had become caught up in the shanghorn-running ceremony on Ty – when he heard a cry of shock or pain behind him. Next second, somebody fell against his back, almost knocking him over. He glanced behind him to see a young Indian man in white shirt, black trousers and black tie sprawl headlong on the dusty ground. The man was holding a brown leather doctor's bag, which was accidentally kicked out of his hand by a panicked member of the passing crowd. Someone else jumped over the man as he tried to rise and caught him a glancing blow on the forehead. The young man went down again, dazed, like a boxer hit by too many punches. People flowed around him, trying not to trample him as he lay on the ground. Behind the stragglers, the Doctor saw that the horse being ridden by the bewhiskered major was heading straight for the stricken man.

The Doctor knew that if he didn't act quickly the horse would trample the man, possibly even kill him. Without hesitation, he darted back through the crowd, slipping between oncoming bodies like a two-legged eel. By the time he reached the man, the horse was no more than a dozen feet away, a galloping wall of solid muscle. The Doctor bent down, grabbed the man under the armpits and dragged him clear – just as the massive charger thundered by in a cloud of dust.

The Doctor bent double, coughing. The young man let out a groan.

'What happened?' he muttered.

'I did,' said the Doctor.

The man raised his head and looked groggily around. The crowd and the pursuing horses had passed now, leaving nothing but hoofmarks, dust, a few trampled turbans and the brown leather doctor's bag, now very much the worse for wear.

'Did you save my life?' the man said with a kind of wonder.

'Suppose I did, yeah,' said the Doctor. 'But you don't have to go over the top about it. I do it a lot. And one display of undying gratitude is very much like another.'

The man looked bemused, either still dazed from his experience or because he wasn't sure how to respond.

To move things along, the Doctor thrust out a hand. 'I'm the Doctor. What's your name?'

'Gopal,' said the young man.

'Nice to meet you, Gopal.' Then the Doctor withdrew the hand and clapped it to his head. 'Oh no!'

'What is it?' asked Gopal, alarmed.

'I've lost my sun visor,' the Doctor said. He looked stricken. 'Aw, I really loved that sun visor. Ginger Spice gave me that.'

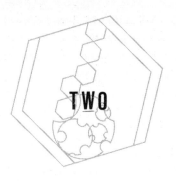

TWO

Cameron Campbell was bored. Bored, bored, bored. There was nothing to do and no one to do it with. Mother and Father would no longer let him out of the house to play with his friends, claiming it was too dangerous to wander the streets; his sister Adelaide seemed to spend all her time over at that stupid camp or asleep in her bed; and his brother Ronny was either too busy with his engineering projects or talking about dull things with their father to ever want to do anything *fun*.

Mother had always told Cameron that he was God's precious gift, that he had come along at a time when she and Father had thought they had done with that sort of thing. That was all very well, but there were times, like now, when Cameron didn't *feel* precious. Instead he felt like a yapping dog who his parents wished would just be quiet and keep out of the way.

He never thought he would say it, but he was actually looking forward to going back to England. Cameron had been born in India and considered it his home, and at first Father's news that they were packing up and heading back to 'Blighty' had filled him with horror. All Cameron knew of England was that it was cold and dreary, that they didn't have bananas and mangoes, and that the only animals were boring things like cats and dogs and sheep. He had initially thought that having to live there would be awful, but now he was starting to change his mind. At least in England he wouldn't be a prisoner in his own home, and Mother had told him that they would have the seaside to visit, and London, and that there would be children his own age to play with.

He would miss his friends here, of course, especially Ranjit... though he hadn't seen Ranjit for a while. That was partly because Mother and Father disapproved of him, and partly – Cameron guessed – because Ranjit had been too busy recently, with his uncle going missing and everything.

In the past, he and Ranjit had always met in secret – either outside the gates of Cameron's school or at the bazaar. But lately, because of the 'troubles', the Campbells' snooty head servant, Becharji, had been taking Cameron to and from school every day, and the bazaar, like almost everywhere else, had been labelled strictly out of bounds.

Sighing, Cameron reached under his bed for his tin of soldiers, intending to set them up for a battle. It wasn't much fun playing on his own, but at least it would while away the half-hour before dinner.

He was pouring them onto the wooden floor when something clattered against his window. He looked up, wondering if it was one of the big flying beetles and whether he could catch it. Then there was another clatter, and this time Cameron saw a number of small stones strike the glass and fall away.

Curious, he walked over to the window. From it he could see the top of the porch, which ran along the side of the house. Yellow light spilled from the porch, illuminating a stretch of hard-baked earth the width of a single-lane road. On the far side of this was a thick clump of bushes, which looked almost black in the encroaching darkness.

At first Cameron saw nothing, and then the bushes parted and a face peered briefly up at him. It was Ranjit! No sooner had he started thinking about his friend than here he was.

Ranjit made a beckoning gesture, and Cameron held up a finger to indicate he would be down in one minute. Soldiers forgotten, he ran out of his room and down the stairs. He could hear Mother, Father and Ronny talking in the drawing room, and crept past the door. Crossing the corridor, he entered the dining room, in which the lamps had been lit and the table set for dinner. He hurried to the back of the room and opened the floor-length glass doors and the screen doors beyond just wide enough to squeeze through.

'Ranjit,' he hissed, standing on the porch and peering into the bushes, 'are you there?'

For a moment he heard nothing but the whirring of cicadas and the gentle croaking of frogs. Then there was a rustle and Ranjit emerged.

Immediately Cameron saw that there was something wrong with his friend. His kurta was grubby and torn and there were dark circles under his eyes, as if he hadn't slept properly in days.

'What's wrong?' Cameron asked.

Ranjit glanced around as if wary of being overheard. 'I'm very afraid.'

'Why?' asked Cameron.

'I believe…' Ranjit raised a hand to his cheek and Cameron saw that it was trembling. 'I believe the world is ending.'

Cameron might have laughed if his friend hadn't looked so serious. 'Why do you believe that?'

'You remember the old temple? The one we play in sometimes? With the monkeys?'

'Yes.'

'I was there last week. I went there to sleep, because it is too dangerous in my uncle's house in the city…'

Haltingly Ranjit told Cameron about the light in the sky and what he had seen in the temple.

For a few moments Cameron simply stared at him. Then he said, 'Are you sure you weren't dreaming?'

'Of course I wasn't,' Ranjit said angrily.

'Maybe it was someone dressed up then? Someone playing a trick.'

Ranjit shook his head. 'It was nothing like that. If you had seen it, you would not be saying these things.'

He seemed to sag a little, and Cameron noticed how thin his friend had become.

'I believe the gods are angry because we are fighting amongst ourselves,' Ranjit said. 'Perhaps Shiva has come to destroy us and start the world anew.'

Cameron thought of the big war that had ended two years before, the war in which his brother, Ronny, had fought. A lot of people they knew had died in that war. Cameron thought if Shiva or any other god was going to destroy the world, he would have done it then.

'I'm sure everything will be fine,' he said. 'Why don't I come to the temple with you tomorrow, and we'll see if Shiva's still there?'

Ranjit looked more hopeful. 'Would you do that?'

'Of course.'

'What time shall we meet?'

Cameron thought about it. Mother had been watching him like a hawk lately. 'Can you be here at dawn? Say, five o'clock in the morning?'

Ranjit nodded, and at that moment the screen doors behind them flew open.

Cameron spun round. Becharji was standing there, immaculate as always in his crisp white jacket and turban. His thin face was like thunder, dark eyes blazing.

'What is going on here?' he demanded.

'Nothing,' said Cameron. 'We were just talking.'

Becharji looked at Ranjit with disdain, his nostrils flaring. 'This boy is an untouchable. You should not talk to such creatures.'

Cameron knew that Becharji was of the Vaisya caste of Indian society, and that he regarded the lower castes as 'untouchables' and not to be fraternised with.

'I don't care about that!' Cameron retorted. 'Ranjit's my friend!'

But Becharji strode forward, making shooing motions, as if Ranjit was a stray chicken which had wandered in from next door. Ranjit backed away, but not quickly enough for Becharji. To Cameron's horror, the servant stooped and picked up a rock. He drew back his arm.

'No!' Cameron shouted. 'You mustn't!'

Becharji threw the rock. Ranjit ducked and it sailed past him, into the bushes. The Indian boy turned and fled. He crashed through the bushes and ran towards the stone wall that encircled the Campbells' property.

He had scrambled up the wall and was straddling the

top when Becharji threw his second rock. This time it hit Ranjit on the side of his head and he disappeared over the wall with a yelp of pain.

'You've hurt him!' Cameron yelled, his face red with fury. 'You might have *killed* him!'

Becharji regarded him coldly. 'I hope so,' he said. 'It will prevent him from returning.'

'I hate you!' Cameron shouted

Before he could say more a voice behind him demanded, 'What's all this noise?'

Cameron turned to see his father standing behind him, his face flushed. 'Becharji threw a rock at my friend!' he wailed. 'It hit him on the *head!*'

Sir Edgar scowled. 'Becharji did *what?*'

Silkily Becharji said, 'A local urchin was trespassing on your property, sahib. I simply threw a rock to drive him away.'

'He threw two rocks!' Cameron cried. 'And the second one hit Ranjit on the head!'

'Well… where's this boy now?' Sir Edgar asked.

'He has gone, sahib,' said Becharji smoothly.

'Yes, well,' said Sir Edgar, 'no harm done then. I'm sure Becharji was only acting for the best.'

'Just so, sahib,' said Becharji, bowing slightly and pressing his hands together.

'But Father—' Cameron protested.

'Let's hear no more about it!' Sir Edgar snapped. 'Now go and spruce yourself up, boy. Dinner will be ready in two ticks.'

Cameron was about to protest further when the jangle of the front door bell resounded through the house.

'What the devil?' said Sir Edgar irritably. 'Visitors at this hour?'

Becharji hurried to open the door. With one last agonised look at the spot where Ranjit had fallen, Cameron hurried after him.

He hung back sullenly as Becharji pulled the door open. Standing outside was a man he recognised, Major Daker, and a woman he did not.

Cameron stared at the woman. She was wearing a flowery dress that was covered in dust, and she had a tangle of bright red hair that fell about her shoulders. Most extraordinary of all, she was wearing a pair of army boots.

'Is your master in?' Major Daker said in his usual brusque way.

Becharji bowed. 'I will fetch him for you, sahib. Please enter.'

Major Daker and the woman stepped into the hall. The woman looked around.

'Where's this then?' she asked.

Major Daker looked as if he didn't like her much. 'This,' he said curtly, 'is the home of Sir Edgar Campbell, the City Magistrate.'

'Oh, brilliant,' the woman said. 'So I'm under arrest,

am I? What for? Minding my own business?'

Cameron gaped. He had never heard a woman talk like this before. The woman saw him and her eyes narrowed.

'What you gawping at, squirt?' she snapped.

Cameron fled.

For a few moments, Ranjit couldn't remember what had happened. All he knew was that he was lying on the ground and that his head hurt. He raised a hand to his temple and it came away wet. Blinking to clear his vision, he saw that his fingertips were red with blood.

As if the shock of seeing the blood had restored his memory, he suddenly recalled the Campbells' servant, Becharji, throwing a rock at him. He supposed Becharji must have thrown a second rock. He hadn't even seen it coming.

Ranjit decided to go to the camp and tell Miss Adelaide what had happened. Perhaps she would punish Becharji. He climbed to his feet, and instantly felt sick and groggy. The world swayed and dipped, and then it began to settle. It was quite a walk to the camp, but he thought he would be all right if he took it slowly.

He managed to keep going for almost half an hour before he collapsed again. He was outside the city limits by this time, walking in the dark along a dusty road, not far from the banks of the Hooghly River. All at once the night-sounds around him seemed to close in, to rise to a booming crescendo inside his head. Ranjit staggered to a halt, and suddenly had the odd sensation that his energy was draining out of his body. Vaguely, he was aware of his legs crumpling beneath him, as if they were made of rotten wood. Then he was lying on the ground, and telling himself that he couldn't sleep, because he would be bitten by snakes or eaten by crocodiles.

Then everything went black.

'Right, better be off,' said the Doctor, grabbing Gopal's hand and shaking it again. 'Things to do, people to find.'

He turned and began to stride away.

'Wait!' Gopal called after him.

The Doctor spun round. 'I absolve you from your debt.'

'What?' said Gopal, confused.

'For saving your life. Don't people usually feel indebted to their saviours? As if they have to offer something in return? But I don't want anything. Oh, unless you've got a chocolate HobNob. Really fancy a chocolate HobNob just now.'

Gopal just stared at him.

'No HobNob?' said the Doctor, sounding a bit disappointed. 'Ah well, never mind. Too much to hope for. Tell you what, just have a magnificent life. Do good things. Make people happy. That'll do me.'

He turned and began to walk away, faster this time. Gopal ran and caught up with him.

'You still here?' said the Doctor, glancing at him. 'Don't you have stuff to do? Like finding a clean shirt, for instance?'

'Who are you looking for?' asked Gopal.

'Friend of mine. She got carried away – literally, I mean, not emotionally.'

'I could help you,' Gopal said.

'Who are *you* then? Head of the Missing Persons Bureau?'

'I am a doctor,' said Gopal proudly.

'Yeah?' said the Doctor. 'Well, good for you, feller. Making people better. Taking their pain away. That's a great thing. But I still think I'll be better on my own.'

'I know Calcutta,' said Gopal, 'and I know that it is not safe for an English gentleman to walk alone at night.'

'I'm not—' the Doctor began, then shook his head. 'Oh, never mind.' He stopped so abruptly that Gopal was a few steps ahead of him before he realised. When Gopal turned back, the Doctor said, 'All right, Gopal, starter for ten. You've got a young... well, young*ish* English woman on her own in Calcutta at night. Where's the most likely place she'll be?'

Gopal considered the question. 'There are several possibilities,' he concluded.

'No time for several,' said the Doctor. 'Just give me numero uno.'

Gopal looked flustered. 'It depends into whose company she has fallen. If she is with your British soldiers, then she will have been taken into protective custody. But if she is with my fellow countrymen... perhaps the camp?'

'What camp's this then?'

'I was on my way there when I became caught up in the mob. It is a place where Muslims and Hindus go who do not wish to fight with one another, but who want simply to live in peace. Many of the people there have fled their homes with few possessions. I'm afraid we have little to offer them, but we do what we can to help the sick and wounded.'

The Doctor stared at Gopal without expression, stared at him so intently that Gopal began to look uncomfortable.

'If Donna's in protective custody,' he said eventually, 'she'll be safe until the morning. So go on then. Show me this camp of yours.'

'It will be my pleasure, Doctor,' Gopal said.

'You honestly think I'm wearing these out of choice?' said Donna. 'Do I *look* like a div?'

Everyone stared at her boots. Mary Campbell, who had made the remark about Donna's unusual choice of footwear, looked as though she had been slapped. Her son, Ronny, on the other hand, covered his mouth as if trying to conceal a smile.

Donna told herself she was coming on a bit strong. But she was riled about the way Daker and this Sir Edgar bloke were treating her, like she was some criminal. It was only natural that she was a bit stroppy – though maybe she was directing it at the wrong person.

'Sorry,' she said grudgingly, 'I'm a bit stressed. It's not every day you get caught up in a riot and arrested, is it?'

Mary Campbell dabbed her nose with a lace handkerchief. 'Quite so,' she said.

'I lost my sandals,' Donna explained, 'so Major Daker lent me these.'

'It was all I could find, I'm afraid,' Daker said.

'Yeah, I don't think he's a flip-flops kinda guy,' Donna said.

Sir Edgar, who Donna thought resembled a bewildered walrus, said gruffly, 'This is getting us nowhere. You still haven't explained what you're doing here, young lady.'

'He brought me,' Donna said, flipping a thumb at Daker.

Sir Edgar went puce. 'I *mean*, what are you doing in Calcutta?'

'I'm here with a friend,' Donna said. 'We're… travelling.'

'Travelling?'

'Yeah, we… we travel. About. From place to place. We're… er… hippies.'

'You're *what?*' spluttered Sir Edgar.

Oops, thought Donna, wrong period.

'It's… um… a new movement. It started in America. Peace, love and understanding. We're seeking spiritual… thingy. Enlightenment. You're gonna hear a lot more about us.'

In about twenty years, she thought.

Sir Edgar closed his eyes briefly. Donna wondered whether she ought to tell him to sit down before he had a heart attack.

'Are you aware, young lady,' he said, 'of the political situation in this country?'

'I am now,' said Donna. 'And I promise I'll be careful.' She looked around. 'Right, are we done? I'll get out of your hair then, shall I?'

She grabbed the arms of the wicker chair in which she was sitting and half-made a move to push herself up. However Major Daker, who was all but standing to attention at her side, placed a restraining hand on her shoulder.

Donna turned her head angrily. 'Don't you manhandle me, mush. I'll have you for assault.'

Ronny laughed. 'Yes, stop bullying our guest, Daker. You too, Father. She's done nothing wrong as far as I can see.'

He caught Donna's eye and winked. She smiled.

'It's for her own good,' said Daker. 'She can't go wandering the streets at night. Lord knows what the coolies will do to her.'

'*Coolies?*' said Donna. 'What hole did you crawl out of? I'll have you know that some of my best mates are from round here. My cousin Janice is married to a Sikh.'

'In Calcutta?' asked Ronny.

'No, Basildon.'

'Good Lord!' exclaimed Mary Campbell.

'That's as may be,' said Sir Edgar, 'but the Major's right. It's not safe out there. We need to find you somewhere to stay.'

'She can stay here, can't she, Father?' said Ronny. 'We've got plenty of room.'

'Well, I…' Sir Edgar blustered, but he got no further. Their discussion was interrupted by a commotion from outside, the voices of several men raised in alarm.

'What the devil's going on now?' Sir Edgar barked. He looked apoplectic at this further disruption to his evening.

'Leave this to me, Sir Edgar,' Daker said, striding across the room to the screen doors that led onto the porch.

Ronny placed his glass of pre-dinner sherry on the mantelpiece and followed the Major.

A moment later, Donna jumped to her feet.

'Where do you think you're going?' Sir Edgar

demanded.

'Outside. You can stand there glugging sherry, but I want to know what's going on.'

She clomped across the room in her army boots and went out through the screen doors.

The first thing she saw was Ronny and Major Daker standing with their backs to her. Something was happening in front of them, but they were blocking her view and she couldn't tell what. She saw servants running about. One of them had a big stick in his hand. Ronny said, 'What a beast. I've never seen anything like it.' Major Daker unclipped the leather holster at his waist and drew out his service revolver.

Donna pushed her way between the two men. Ronny glanced at her, surprised. 'I really think you ought to go back inside, Miss Noble.'

'No way,' she said – and then she saw what everyone was looking at. 'Oh my God.'

It was a crocodile. But it was unlike any crocodile Donna had seen before. It was huge for a start, at least eight metres from nose to tail. It was smeared in dark green slime, and its vast scaly bulk was covered in bony black growths and protuberances, which had twisted its body, making it look more like a gnarled and ancient tree branch than a living creature. It propelled itself with a sideways, almost crab-like motion, and as one of the servants darted forward and hit it with a stick, it swung its huge head round, opened its jaws wide and snapped at him, just missing him as he jumped back.

Donna shuddered at the sight of its vicious teeth, and a glimpse of more of the horrible growths inside its grey-pink gullet.

'What's wrong with it?' she said, clutching Ronny's arm.

'I hardly think that's our concern,' barked Daker.

As if the crocodile had heard him, it rolled its oily yellow eye in their direction and suddenly swung round, its massive jaws opening.

Daker didn't hesitate. He fired several shots straight into the creature's gaping mouth. It shuddered as the bullets hit it, but it kept on coming. Donna and Ronny leaped back, but the Major stood his ground. He fired at the creature again and again. Each bullet slowed it down a little more, until finally it crashed down dead on the wooden boards, its snout no more than a metre from Daker's feet.

For a few moments, as the echoes of the gunshots faded into the night, there was a stunned silence.

Then Donna said, 'That kind of thing normal for round here, is it?'

THREE

'I have never seen a man look so angry and so sad before,' Gopal said.

The Doctor's eyes flickered to regard him. For a long moment he didn't speak. Then he said, 'I've seen more suffering in my life than you can possibly imagine. But that doesn't mean it ever gets any easier. Sometimes I can't help thinking I've lived too long.'

'But you are just a young man,' Gopal said.

The Doctor didn't reply.

They were walking through the camp, through crowds of exhausted, emaciated people. Many were sitting around fires, talking quietly or muttering in prayer or simply staring into the flames. Some were sleeping on the open ground, using nothing but their own hands as a pillow. A few were eating, taking their time over their small portions of food.

The Doctor felt someone tugging at his jacket. A small boy was staring up at him with big brown eyes, hand outstretched.

The Doctor crouched down. 'Hello,' he said. 'What's your name?'

If the boy was surprised to hear the Doctor speaking in his own language he didn't show it. 'Jivraj,' he said shyly.

'Right then, Jivraj,' the Doctor said, reaching into his jacket pocket, 'let's see what we can find.'

He produced a satsuma and handed it to the boy. Jivraj grinned. Then he produced a pair of chattering wind-up teeth and showed Jivraj how they worked. Jivraj laughed delightfully, and ran off to show the gifts to his family.

'There are hundreds of boys like Jivraj in this camp,' said Gopal. 'If only we had food for all of them.'

It took several minutes to reach the trio of medical tents that had been set up in the centre of the camp. When they arrived, Gopal asked a young Indian orderly where they could find Dr Morgan and was informed that he was in the isolation tent.

'Isolation?' said the Doctor.

'A number of people have arrived at the camp this week with symptoms that are proving most mysterious.'

'Mysterious in what way?'

When Gopal told him, the Doctor raised an eyebrow and tilted his chin back. 'I think you'd better show me,' he said.

Gopal led the Doctor to the tent at the end of the row, holding open the flap so that he could enter.

There was a woman in the tent, tending the sick, a well-dressed English woman in her early twenties, her chestnut hair tied in a bun. She turned to see who had entered, wafting at the flies above her head. Her eyes widened when she saw the Doctor.

'Hello, Gopal,' she said, though her gaze remained fixed on the Doctor, who was looking around, taking everything in. 'Who's your friend?'

'This is… the Doctor,' Gopal said.

'Well, we can never have enough of those,' said the woman. 'Have you come to help us, Dr…?'

'Just Doctor,' the Doctor said, flashing her a smile.

'Very mysterious,' said the woman.

'Like a lot of things round here.' The Doctor nodded at the muslin partition. 'I gather the "special" patients are through there? Mind if I take a look?'

'Well, I… er… perhaps we ought to clear it with Edward first.'

'Clear what with Edward?' said a voice at the entrance of the tent.

The Doctor turned and saw a young man in a grubby doctor's coat, who looked as if he had barely slept or eaten in days.

He sprang across, hand outstretched. 'Dr Morgan!' he exclaimed. 'Pleasure to meet you! Brilliant work you're doing! I was just saying to… er…'

'Adelaide,' said the young woman.

'… to Adelaide here that I wouldn't mind taking a quick squiz at the special patients. In fact, that's why I'm here. Dr John Smith, Royal College of Surgeons, Rare and Tropical Diseases Unit.'

With the hand that wasn't vigorously shaking the bemused Dr Morgan's, the Doctor dipped into the pocket of his jacket and produced his psychic paper, which he flashed to each of them in turn.

Gopal said, 'You are a man of continual surprises, Dr Smith.'

'Aren't I just?' said the Doctor. 'Never hurts to keep people on their toes, that's my motto.'

'But… how did you find out about our patients?' Edward asked. 'I've only just…'

'Information superhighway,' said the Doctor quickly, and clapped his hands together. 'Right, let's get cracking. Time and tide, and all that.' He crossed to the muslin partition and reached out for it. Then abruptly he cried, 'Ah!' and spun back round, causing Edward, Adelaide and Gopal to jump back.

'First things first. My friend Donna's not here, is she? Long red hair? Shouts a lot?'

Edward and Adelaide exchanged a glance. Both shook their heads.

'Ah well, never mind,' said the Doctor. 'I'm sure she'll turn up. Come on then. Allons-y.'

He swished through the partition before anyone could advise him to wear a face-mask. He walked along the row, looking at each of the patients in turn. Finally he whipped out his sonic screwdriver, pointed it at the nearest patient and turned it on.

'Whatever is that device?' asked Edward, astonished.

'Diagnostic wand,' said the Doctor. 'It's a new thing. Still in the experimental stage. All very hush-hush, so don't tell anyone.'

He held the sonic up and appeared to sniff it. Suddenly his face went very serious.

'What is it?' asked Adelaide.

'Cellular disruption. This is very bad. There's only one thing which can have caused this.'

'Which is?' asked Edward.

'Zytron energy. But that's impossible. It won't be discovered on Earth for another three thousand years.'

Edward, Adelaide and Gopal all looked at each other. Tentatively, Edward said, 'How can you possibly—'

'Shush,' said the Doctor, holding up a hand. 'I'm thinking.' He stared into the middle distance, tapping the now silent sonic against his bottom lip. 'So who uses unshielded zytron energy in the twentieth century? Whoever they are, they're not from round here.' His gaze scorched across the confused trio standing in front of him. 'Anything else happened recently? Any odd occurrences, strange rumours, peculiar lights in the sky?'

Adelaide said, 'Well—' but Edward cut her off with a scowl.

'Let's stick to facts, shall we, and not muddy the water with silly stories.'

The Doctor glanced at him. 'Oh, it's amazing how many facts you can find hidden in silly stories. Go on, Adelaide.'

A little self-consciously she said, 'About a week ago, there were strange colours in the night sky. We all saw them – you too, Edward.'

'Atmospheric disturbance of some kind,' Edward said grumpily. 'Nothing supernatural about that.'

'Maybe,' said the Doctor, 'but what *caused* the disturbance, eh?'

Gopal, who had been silent for a while, said, 'Some people say they saw a shooting star fall to earth that night.'

'Do they?' said the Doctor, as if this was significant. 'What else?'

Adelaide felt uncomfortable at the inference that they were holding back. Still scowling, Edward said, 'What you must understand about India, Dr Smith, is that these are volatile times and, for all the advances that have been made in the past few decades, the majority of the population remain poor, uneducated and highly superstitious.'

'Thank you. I'll bear that in mind,' the Doctor said flatly. 'You were saying, Adelaide?'

Adelaide wasn't aware she had been saying anything, but under the Doctor's scrutiny, she found herself blurting, 'A great many people have gone missing recently, Dr Smith. Undoubtedly, most of them have fled, or have even been killed by their fellow countrymen—'

'Their bodies are thrown into the river for the crocodiles to dispose of,' added Gopal, earning a disapproving glance from Edward.

'But nevertheless,' Adelaide continued, 'the city has recently been rife with talk of "half-made men", who come in the night and steal people away. A lady called Apala, whom I spoke to only yesterday, is adamant that her husband was abducted by these creatures. She claims she saw them, clear as day.'

'Does she now?' the Doctor murmured. Edward snorted.

'Wild stories,' he said. 'Arrant nonsense.'

'Oh yeah, bound to be,' said the Doctor airily. 'Even so, I wouldn't mind a quick chinwag with Apala. I mean, without knowing that she knows, she might know something that'll help us, and there's no knowing without asking. Right, Gopal?'

'Er… yes,' Gopal said.

'Lovely jubbly,' said the Doctor. 'So what are we all standing around jabbering for? Adelaide, you come with me. Edward and Gopal, you go and make people better.'

He swept out of the tent, Adelaide hurrying after him. She could only remember roughly where Apala had set up her shelter, and it took several minutes of searching before they found her.

She was sitting cross-legged outside her lean-to, feeding a carefully swaddled baby by using her finger to scoop what looked like semolina from a small wooden bowl. Her sari, a shimmering blue edged with gold trim, might once have been grand but was now dull with wear. Apala's face was thinner and more angular than it should have been. Hunger had sharpened her cheekbones.

The Doctor squatted down and smiled at her. Back in the tent, his dark gaze had been unsettling, but Adelaide was now struck by how warm and gentle his smile was.

'Hi, Apala,' he said, 'I'm the Doctor. What's your daughter's name?' He stretched out a long index finger and the tiny baby curled its fist around it.

The woman seemed too weary to be surprised that the Doctor was speaking her language. 'Manu,' she said quietly.

'She's beautiful,' said the Doctor, and Apala's face broke into a smile. In the same quiet voice he asked,

'Will you tell me about the half-made men, Apala? About how they took your husband away?'

The smile slipped from her face, but after a moment's hesitation she nodded. 'My husband and I were sleeping,' she said. 'I heard him cry out and I came awake at once. In the moonlight shining through the window I saw him struggling with two men. I called out his name, but before he could respond all three of them vanished, like morning mist.'

'And what did these men look like?'

Apala raised a hand, bracelets jangling on her bony wrist, and touched her shawled head. 'They had no hair. And their skin was completely white, like salt.' She shivered. 'And where their eyes should have been, there were only shadows.'

'Thank you,' the Doctor said gently, 'you've been a great help. And I promise you, Apala, I'll do everything I can to get your husband back.'

He stood up.

'What did she tell you?' asked Adelaide.

'Enough to make me suspect that my stay will be longer than I thought. I should have brought my jim-jams.'

Just then a ripple seemed to go through the crowd, a palpable wave of excitement. One by one, people began to stand up, to crane their necks, to point into the darkness. The murmur rose into a buzz of chatter, which then became a chant. The chant was weak and ragged at first, but it was quickly taken up, until eventually people were clapping their hands and shouting with gusto.

'What's happening? What are they saying?' Adelaide asked, looking around in puzzlement.

A slow grin was spreading across the Doctor's face. 'They're saying "Bapu ki jai". It means "Long live the Father". Look.'

He pointed towards a moving knot of people in the centre of the crowd. Adelaide narrowed her eyes, trying to focus through the fire-lit darkness. At the head of the crowd, walking towards them, was a little, bald, bespectacled man wrapped in a simple white robe and carrying a gnarled walking stick.

'My goodness,' Adelaide said, clearly a little awe-struck, 'is that who I think it is?'

'Oh yes,' said the Doctor, his grin widening. 'Mohandas "Mahatma" Gandhi, as I live and breathe.'

'Wee dram, sir?' said Captain McMahon, holding up a bottle.

Major Daker settled back into his favourite chair in the officers' mess. 'Don't mind if I do, McMahon.' He closed his eyes and sighed deeply.

'Been a tough one today, sir,' McMahon said.

Daker grunted, removed his peaked cap and wiped sweat from his brow. 'You're telling me.'

McMahon poured the drinks and brought them

across. 'Your good health, sir.'

'And yours.'

They each took a sip, reflecting on the day's events. For a few moments all was silent apart from the lazy swish of the ceiling fan overhead and the soft chorus of insect sounds drifting through the wire-mesh screens across the open windows.

Eventually Daker stirred and said, 'I don't mind telling you, McMahon, I've just about had it with this country. The writing's on the wall for the British in India now. The sooner we can all go home and leave the Indians to it, the better.'

'Couldn't agree more, sir,' McMahon said. He noticed Daker wince and touch a spot behind his left ear. 'Are you all right, sir?'

'Touch of heatstroke,' Daker said. 'Either that or I've been bitten by something.' He snorted. 'Another reason for looking forward to going home, eh, McMahon? The good old British weather.'

'Oh yes, sir,' said McMahon. 'Can't tell you how much I'm looking forward to the Highland rain.'

The two men chuckled. But no sooner had they raised their glasses to their lips again than the peace of the night was disturbed by shouting. Next moment they saw several men run past the window, most dressed in the British Army's regulation nightwear of white singlets and shorts.

Daker jerked to his feet so violently that he spilled

his drink. 'What the devil is happening now?'

Someone pounded on the door of the mess. McMahon put his drink down and hurried across the room to open it.

Bathed in the powerful night-lights that shone across the barrack grounds were a huddle of army privates, most of whom had evidently just been roused from sleep. The squaddies were all in their late teens or early twenties, though at that moment, hair awry and eyes wide, they looked like a bunch of schoolboys scared witless by spooky stories.

'What's the meaning of this?' Daker bellowed, his face reddening. 'Get back to your beds at once!'

One of the young privates stepped forward.

'Begging your pardon, sir, but… well, it's Tommy Fox and Alfred Swift, sir. They've been taken.'

'*Taken?*' Daker repeated in a strangled voice. 'What in God's name are you babbling about, Wilkins?'

Private Wilkins glanced at his colleagues, who offered silent encouragement with nods and raised eyebrows. Wilkins said, 'Well, sir, my bed is next to Tommy's, sir. I heard a noise and woke up to see someone standing by his bed. I sat up, and that's when I noticed another figure, leaning over Alf's bed. I shouted out, which woke up a few of the other lads, sir. And then there was this… sort of flash. And the next second the two figures had gone, but so had Tommy and Alf. Their beds were just… empty.'

Behind Wilkins the other soldiers were nodding. One of them, a square-set private with pock-marked cheeks, said, 'It's true, sir, every word. I saw the figures too. And I also saw them disappear, sir. They just vanished into thin air, taking Tommy and Alf with them.'

'*Preposterous!*' barked Daker.

In a calmer voice, McMahon asked, 'What did these figures look like?'

Again Wilkins glanced at his colleagues. 'Well, sir, they… they looked like ghosts.'

'*Ghosts?*' exclaimed Daker.

'Yes, sir. They were white, sir. Chalky white. And their faces were… sort of unfinished, sir.' He shuddered.

'And you were so frightened that you ran like children!' sneered Daker. 'A dozen members of His Majesty's so-called elite fighting force. It's an utter disgrace. You should be ashamed of yourselves.'

'Yes, sir,' Wilkins mumbled. 'Only…'

'Only what? Spit it out, private,' ordered McMahon.

'Well, sir, we… we didn't run when the figures vanished, sir. We ran when they came back.'

'What?' Daker snapped. 'You mean these damned "ghosts" of yours are still there?'

'They… they might be, sir.'

'Well, why didn't you say so in the first place, you stupid boy?' Not for the first time that day Daker drew his service revolver. 'Come on, McMahon, let's sort this out. You lot wait inside. I'll deal with you later.'

He stalked off, McMahon in tow. The squaddies' sleeping quarters were behind the main HQ building and administration offices, in a dozen wooden huts arranged in twin rows of six. Each hut contained sixteen beds, eight on each side, with a narrow central aisle. The hut from which Wilkins and his colleagues had fled was on the second row on the far right. It was the hut that was closest to (though still some distance from) the perimeter fence. Behind the huts a carpet of thick undergrowth led to a dense screen of bamboo trees.

As Daker and McMahon bypassed the first row of huts and approached the second, they saw that the door to the now-empty hut was gaping open. A light above the door threw a pool of illumination onto the ground.

'I would advise caution, sir,' said McMahon as Daker strode brazenly forward, revolver at the ready.

'Don't tell me you believe this ridiculous ghost story, McMahon,' Daker retorted, making no attempt to lower his voice.

'Not as such, sir, though it seems likely enough that we've had intruders of some kind.'

'If they're made of flesh and blood, then I'd like to see them try to defy a bullet.'

'They might be armed themselves, sir,' McMahon pointed out.

'Hmph,' Daker said, though he changed direction and skirted the pool of light, using the shadows as cover. McMahon approached the door from the opposite side, his gun also drawn. When the two officers were pressed against the wooden wall on either side of the doorway, Daker nodded and pointed at himself, mouthing, 'Me first.' The instant McMahon nodded, Daker went in, fast and low, gun held out before him.

The hut was empty, and aside from two rows of beds which had evidently been vacated in a hurry, there was nothing to suggest that anything untoward had occurred. Both officers examined the beds of the men who had allegedly vanished. The sheets were rumpled, and a pillow from one of the beds had fallen to the floor, but there were no other signs of a struggle – no muddy footprints, no bloodstains, nothing damaged or knocked over.

Daker frowned. 'What do you think, McMahon? Mass hysteria?'

McMahon shrugged. 'Could be, sir, but these lads are pretty level-headed. Plus it still doesn't account for the disappearance of Fox and Swift.'

'Hmm,' said Daker. 'Perhaps we'd better have a quick poke about outside. You head east, I'll head west. We'll move inwards and meet in the middle.'

'Understood, sir.'

The two men vacated the hut and headed off in opposite directions. Most of the fenced area housing the army barracks was well-lit at night, though the sizeable patch of ground behind the huts was cloaked in shadow. Daker again rubbed at the sore spot behind his ear. The skin felt raised there, as if some insect had bitten him. Typical if he contracted something nasty less than a month before he was due to head home.

Aside from the endless racket of frogs and insects, the night was quiet. None of the sleeping occupants of the other huts seemed to have been bothered by the so-called 'ghosts'. In truth, Daker half-expected to stumble across the two missing privates in the thick undergrowth behind the huts. Perhaps they were playing a prank on their mates, or maybe one had been sleepwalking and wandered off, and the other had gone looking for him. Inexplicable as the soldiers' story seemed, Daker felt sure there would be a reasonable explanation. It could even be that a couple of coolies had painted themselves white and kidnapped the young men with a view to holding them for ransom, or in revenge for what they claimed were the British Army's heavy-handed tactics during the recent troubles. If so, Daker would find the perpetrators and come down hard on them. He tightened his grip on his revolver, as if he already had them in his sights.

He moved methodically through the undergrowth behind the huts, wary of snakes. He peered hard at every shadow, trying to remain alert, though the heat seemed greater back here, as if the thick, fleshy leaves of the plants had soaked it up during the day and were now releasing it in waves. As a result, his thoughts felt slow and muzzy; the patch behind his ear itched.

He snapped back to full attention when he heard a cry, followed by a gunshot.

'McMahon,' Daker shouted and ran towards the sound. It was hard going through the thick foliage, but less than ten seconds later he rounded a clump of flowering bushes and saw, fifty yards ahead, McMahon grappling with two men. Shouting the captain's name a second time, Daker ran towards the trio. He was no more than twenty yards away when there was a silvery shimmer in the air, like the ripple of a heat haze on a summer's day, and suddenly there was only one man standing where three had been a second before.

Daker was so shocked that he stumbled and almost fell to his knees. Recovering himself, he pointed his gun at the lone figure.

'Hands in the air,' he ordered.

The figure did not respond.

'Hands in the air or I fire.'

Instead of obeying, the figure began to walk purposefully towards him. As it emerged from the shadows, Daker saw that it was stripped to the waist, wearing nothing but a pair of loose salwar pants, of a type similar to those favoured by many Indians. However, one thing was instantly clear to the Major: this was no local man. The closer it got to him, the more he began to doubt that the creature was even human.

It was man-*shaped*, certainly, but its skin was a ghastly, fish-belly white, and perfectly smooth and hairless, like polished marble. Even more unsettling was its face, which had the hideously blank expression of a death-mask. It was not until the creature was just a few yards away, however, that Daker became aware of the most horrifying detail of all.

The thing had no eyes. Where its eyes *should* have been there were nothing but smooth hollows filled with grey shadow.

'*Halt!*' He almost screamed the word this time. The figure, though, simply kept on coming. In a feverish panic Daker fired. The gun roared and he saw a neat black hole appear in the creature's chest. It staggered back a few steps, then straightened up.

Daker fired again. A second hole appeared a few inches to the right of the first. Once again the figure staggered, then straightened. It stood for a moment, as if contemplating its next move – and then Daker became aware of another strange silvery shimmer. For a moment he was blinded, as if he had walked out of a darkened room into the smeary glare of the sun. When he blinked the light from his eyes a moment later, the creature was gone.

Adelaide stepped forward. 'Mr Gandhi,' she said, a

tremor in her voice.

The little man came to a halt and smiled. People were still crowding around him, but no one was pushing or shoving. They all seemed content to wait their turn to touch his sandalled feet, or his arm, or his simple homespun robe. Some even seemed happy merely to touch his footprints in the dust.

Gandhi pressed his palms together in the traditional Hindu greeting and nodded first to Adelaide and then to the Doctor. They returned the greeting, the Doctor making no attempt to hide the soppy smile on his face.

'It's… a pleasure to meet you, sir,' Adelaide stammered.

'Oh, and quite definitely an honour,' added the Doctor, stepping forward. 'And I know you're not into being idolised and all that, which, ironically, is one of the most brilliant things about you, but can I just say, for the record, cos this might be my only chance, that you, Mr Mohandas Gandhi, are one of *the* most amazing human beings who has ever lived, and who ever *will* live, and for my money you're right up there with Will Shakespeare, Mother Teresa and Arthur Thorndike, the janitor from Basingstoke, who… oh, hang on, scratch that, he hasn't been born yet.' He opened his mouth to say more, but then caught Adelaide's eye and grinned sheepishly. 'Whoops, sorry. Babbling a bit. Always get like that when I'm overexcited. Ooh, still doing it. Sorry. OK, finished now.'

He closed his mouth and pulled his fingers across his lips in a zipping motion.

Gandhi bowed again and said, 'Thank you for your greeting. Your words greatly honour me – but I'm afraid I don't deserve them.'

'Course you do,' said the Doctor, 'but let's not bang on about it. I know what fans can be like. Except, can I just say, the Salt March in 1930… brilliant. Stroke of genius.'

Gandhi smiled. 'Actually, what I did was a very ordinary thing. I simply let the British know that they could not order me about in my own country.'

'Yeah, but it was the *way* you did it,' said the Doctor. 'Non-violent, non-confrontational, non-cooperation. Amazing.'

'Forgive me,' said Adelaide, 'but what *was* the Salt March?'

The Doctor boggled at her. 'Where have you been living? On the moon?'

Adelaide blushed. 'Oh, I'm aware of Mr Gandhi, and of his ongoing campaign. But I was only five years old in 1930, Dr Smith. I'm afraid my knowledge of the details of Mr Gandhi's early life are a little rusty.'

'Sorry,' said the Doctor, realising he had embarrassed Adelaide. 'Didn't mean to be rude. The British declared it illegal for Indians to possess salt from anywhere other than the government's salt monopoly – which was grossly unfair. After all, salt's an abundant, readily available mineral. Why should people who have barely got two grains of rice to rub together have to pay for it? So Mohandas and a few of his mates… oh, do you mind if I call you Mohandas?'

Gandhi laughed delightedly. 'Not at all. First names are an indicator of friendship, are they not?'

'Yes,' said the Doctor, grinning. 'Yes, they are.'

'In which case, we should tell you ours,' said Adelaide. 'This is Dr John Smith and I'm Adelaide Campbell.'

'But all my *best* friends just call me Doctor,' said the Doctor quickly, and went on without a pause, 'so anyway Mohandas here walked across India, picking up followers along the way. He walked two hundred miles in twenty-four days, all the way from Sabarmati to the coast at Dandi. By the time he got there, he had thousands of people with him. He went down to the beach and picked up a handful of salt that had been left by the tide. It was a brilliantly simple act of defiance against a stupid rule, and it riveted the whole of India. Millions followed his example. Right across the country, people of all castes started to make and sell their own salt. A hundred thousand were arrested and imprisoned. The authorities couldn't cope. Within a few weeks of Mohandas picking up those few grains of salt, the whole of India was in revolt.'

The Doctor came to a breathless halt, his eyes shining. Gandhi regarded him like a kindly and indulgent uncle.

Quietly he said, 'I regret to say that my action caused the needless deaths of many people.'

'But that wasn't your fault,' said the Doctor. 'And their deaths weren't needless surely? They died fighting for a cause, for something they believed in.'

Gandhi shook his head slowly. 'There is an important distinction to be made here, Doctor. I will happily die for what I believe is a just cause, but I will not die fighting for it. To die in anger and conflict makes a man no better than his opponent. It has always been my belief that if an opponent strikes you on your right cheek, you should offer him your left. This shows him that you are courageous enough to take a blow, but that you will not fight back. This in turn diminishes your attacker. It makes his hatred for you decrease and his respect increase.'

The Doctor nodded. 'But what happens when you come up against an opponent who is incapable of respect? What happens when your opponent *can* only hate? What happens if by killing the one you can save the many?'

Gandhi seemed oddly pleased that this stranger was questioning his beliefs. He pondered a moment, taking his time to answer. 'Then I suppose you must die in the knowledge that at least you have remained as merciful and pure as it is possible for a flesh-and-blood creature to be. And while your opponent may have triumphed physically, spiritually he will be empty, and that is something he will be forced to address in the fullness of time.'

The Doctor's face had become sombre. 'I've spent a great deal of my life fighting for what I believe is a just cause too, Mohandas. I've seen so much injustice, so much bloodshed, that I sometimes think I'll never wash the stain of it from my hands. I used to be so forgiving, but now…' He shook his head and looked away.

'And yet I sense that you always do what you think is right, Doctor, that you sail turbulent seas and try your utmost to maintain a consistent course?'

The Doctor stared across the mass of faces in front of him, the people who were gathered patiently around the little man in the homespun robe. The sudden look of brooding intensity in his eyes drew a shudder from Adelaide. She got the impression that the Doctor was seeing and yet not seeing the people before him, that his horizons were more distant than hers would ever be.

Suddenly he smiled. 'It's true what they say about you, Mohandas.'

Gandhi raised his eyebrows good-humouredly. 'Oh?'

'They say a conversation with you is a voyage of discovery. They say you dare to go anywhere without a chart.'

Gandhi chuckled. 'As do you, I think, Doctor.'

'Oh yeah,' said the Doctor. 'Why go somewhere

you've already been when there's a whole universe to explore?'

The two men laughed, and the people around them dutifully laughed too. As the laughter faded, the Doctor and Adelaide heard a shout from behind them. 'Bapu! Bapu!'

They turned to see a small figure running through the camp from the direction of the medical tents. At first, in the darkness, it appeared the boy was wearing a turban, but as he drew closer, the Doctor realised that his head had been dressed and bandaged.

'Hello, Ranjit,' said Adelaide as the boy reached them, panting. 'What happened to you?'

'Hurt my head. Some soldiers found me and brought me here.' Ranjit turned to Gandhi. 'Bapu, please. I must speak to you.'

'Then speak,' Gandhi said, patient as ever.

Ranjit eyed the crowd uncertainly. 'I must speak to you *in private*, Bapu.'

Gandhi smiled. 'But we are all friends here. Surely friends should have no secrets from one another?'

Ranjit stepped closer to Gandhi, close enough to murmur into his ear.

'Bapu, last week I saw a light fall from the sky. It fell into a temple not far from here. When I entered the temple…' he shuddered '… I saw *him*, Bapu.'

Before Gandhi could reply, the Doctor, who had been listening to Ranjit's account, leaned forward.

'Who did you see?' he asked quietly.

Ranjit glanced from Gandhi to the Doctor, fear on his face. 'I saw Shiva,' he whispered. 'I saw him with my own eyes.'

There was a moment of silence. The Doctor leaned back, looking thoughtful.

'I think I'd like to see this temple,' he murmured.

FOUR

By 5.20, there was still no sign of Ranjit. Cameron didn't know whether to be annoyed or concerned that his friend hadn't turned up. Maybe after yesterday he was too frightened to return to the house. Or maybe he had been so badly hurt that he was now lying in a coma somewhere, or wandering around, unable to remember who he was.

At least he wasn't still lying on the other side of the wall. Cameron had sneaked out of the house after dinner last night to check. He was still annoyed that he had missed all the excitement with the crocodile. He had come running from his bedroom when he had heard the gunshots, but Mother had refused to allow him to go outside. Ronny had taken him for a sneaky look later, though. The servants had moved the crocodile off the porch and into the shed, and had put a sheet over it to keep the flies off.

Cameron could see straight away that there had been something wrong with it. It was the biggest crocodile he had ever seen, but it had been twisted and covered with weird black lumps. Cameron had asked Ronny what they were going to do with it.

'Becharji says his cousin has a lorry. He's promised to come by and pick the beast up tomorrow,' Ronny had replied.

'And what will Becharji's cousin do with it?' Cameron had asked.

'He'll probably chuck it in the river or burn it,' Ronny told him. 'Just as long as he takes it away, he can make it into handbags for all I care,'

Cameron looked again at the big grandfather clock ticking away the minutes in the otherwise silent hallway. It was now 5.25 – still dark outside, but in half an hour the servants would be getting up to prepare breakfast for the family.

All at once Cameron rose from his perch at the bottom of the stairs. It seemed that Ranjit wasn't coming, which meant he had one of two choices: either he could abandon the expedition, or he could go on alone.

The prospect of exploring the old temple on his own was a pretty scary one (as was the thought of the trouble he would find himself in when his parents found out), but Cameron knew there was no way he could go back to bed and forget about it. He hadn't been outside in ages, and had been looking forward to this morning's adventure so much that last night he had barely been able to sleep.

Before his nerve could fail him, therefore, he padded to the kitchen and picked up his knapsack of provisions. There was food in there and water, plus his trusty catapult, which he'd spent hours practising with in the back garden, and which he would use to frighten the monkeys away if they turned nasty.

With his knapsack on his back, he crept into the hallway and let himself out of the house. Now all he had to do was pick up his bicycle from the shed, where the dead crocodile lay waiting for collection, and his adventure could begin.

'Five more minutes, Mum,' Donna groaned as someone knocked on the door. Then she remembered where she was and snapped awake.

India! She was in India! For a moment she felt a giddy sense of excitement, a sense of disbelief that this was actually her life. It was a feeling she often had nowadays, first thing in the morning, just after she woke up. She relished the fact that every day she spent with the Doctor was an incredible voyage of discovery.

First things first, though. Out of bed, washed,

dressed, breakfast. She looked at the clothes Mary Campbell had lent her, which apparently belonged to her daughter. Mary was all repressed and buttoned-up, but her daughter Adelaide had obviously made more of an effort to integrate with the locals. Ten minutes later Donna came downstairs in a silky plum-coloured dress, which wasn't a bad fit, although a tiny bit tight in the hip area.

The first person she saw was Ronny, suited and booted, about to enter the dining room for breakfast.

'Oi, Ronny,' she hissed to attract his attention.

He turned and smiled. 'Good morning, Donna.'

'Hiya. Listen, Ronny, be honest,' she said in a low voice. 'Does my bum look big in this?'

She gave him a twirl, and when she turned to face him again saw that he was blushing.

'You… er… look quite delightful,' he stammered.

'Really? You're not just saying that? Cos I want you to be honest. Well… honest*ish*.'

Ronny laughed. 'I can honestly say, Donna, that I've never met a girl quite like you.'

'Yeah? You wanna come down the Dog and Trumpet on a Saturday night. They're *all* like me in there.'

He tilted an elbow in her direction and said in his plummiest tones, 'Would you do me the honour of accompanying me to breakfast, Miss Noble?'

Donna slipped a hand into the crook of his elbow. 'Don't mind if I do, squire.'

They entered the dining room. Bright sunlight was falling across the pristine white tablecloth, flashing off the white china plates and silver cutlery. A turbaned servant stepped forward and pulled out a chair for Donna to sit down, then he shook out a napkin and draped it across her lap.

Sir Edgar and Mary Campbell were already seated at the table. Sir Edgar was reading *The Times,* having already polished off a large fried breakfast. When he lowered the paper to grunt good morning, Donna noticed that he had egg yolk in his moustache.

'Morning, all,' said Ronny, and glanced around. 'Where's Cameron this morning?'

'Still in bed, I expect,' said Sir Edgar. 'Lazy blighter. If he doesn't turn up soon, he'll miss breakfast.'

Ronny winked at Donna. 'Leave him be, Father. It *is* Saturday. He's probably exhausted after all the excitement last night.'

'Did you sleep well, dear?' Mary asked Donna. She was picking at a slice of buttered toast like a bird.

'Yeah, lovely, thanks,' Donna said. 'I don't think I've ever slept in a four-poster before.' Then she reconsidered. 'No, I tell a lie. There was one in the hotel we stayed in after my cousin Janice's hen night. Mind you, I was plastered, so I don't remember much about it.'

There was a shocked silence. Ronny said quickly, 'Doesn't Donna look beautiful in Adelaide's dress, Mother?'

'Very nice,' said Mary in a tight voice.

From the hallway came the sound of the front door opening and a woman's voice called, 'Yoo-hoo!'

'Speak of the devil,' said Ronny. 'We're in here, Addie.'

The dining room door opened and a pretty girl with chestnut hair entered. She looked at Donna in surprise, but her smile was friendly enough.

'Hello,' she said. 'Do you know, I've got a dress exactly like that.'

'It *is* yours,' said Donna with a grimace of apology. 'I kind of borrowed it.'

'Donna arrived last night in rather unusual circumstances,' said Ronny. 'Sit down and have a cup of tea, Addie, and I'll tell you all about it.'

A servant stepped forward to pull out a spare chair for Adelaide. She dropped into it with a grateful groan.

'Tough night?' said Donna.

Adelaide nodded. 'But an eventful one. We've had some rather amazing visitors at the refugee camp where I work. In fact, I'm still buzzing with excitement. I doubt I'll be able to sleep.' She leaned across and rubbed Ronny's hand affectionately. 'But I'm being rude. Tell me your news first, Ronny. I want to hear all about Donna. Pleased to meet you, Donna, by the way.'

She held out a hand, which Donna shook. Donna

decided that she liked Adelaide immediately. She was certainly much friendlier than her dried-up old sour-puss of a mother.

Adelaide's eyes sparkled as she listened to Ronny recount the tale of Donna's arrival and the attack by the monstrous crocodile.

'My goodness,' she said. 'So where is this friend of yours, Donna?'

'Yes, we never got to the bottom of that, did we?' said Sir Edgar, with a frown.

Donna shrugged. 'I dunno where he is, but I've got to find him. I mean, thanks for putting me up, but he's my passport out of here.'

'What's his name?' asked Ronny. 'With all of Father's contacts, I'm sure somebody will know where he is.'

Donna said awkwardly, 'Well, he doesn't really use a name. He calls himself the Doctor.'

Adelaide jerked upright in her seat. 'I don't believe it! He's one of the men I was going to tell you about. He turned up at the camp last night. He said his name was Dr John Smith.'

'Yeah, that's the name he… I mean… yeah, that's him,' said Donna, jumping to her feet.

Ronny looked at her, perplexed. 'Aren't you having any breakfast?'

'No time,' Donna said, and turned back to Adelaide. 'So how do I get to this camp of yours?'

***

'Hello, Mr Doctor.'

The Doctor looked over his shoulder to see Ranjit standing at the entrance to the tent, grinning at him.

'Hiya, Ranjit,' he said. 'How's the old noggin?'

Ranjit touched the bandage around his head. 'The noggin is fine, Mr Doctor. How are you?'

'Oh, coping, you know. Been helping out a bit here and there. Keeping busy.'

'Have you been making people better with your magic torch?' Ranjit asked.

The Doctor switched the sonic off and straightened up from the patient he had been examining. He slipped the sonic into the inside pocket of his jacket, then took off his black-framed spectacles, folded them up, and slipped them into the opposite inside pocket.

'Not curing so much as diagnosing,' he said, 'which means—'

'I know,' said Ranjit. 'Finding out what's wrong with them. Correct?'

'Correct,' said the Doctor, impressed.

'Haven't you been to sleep?' Ranjit asked.

'Nah, what would I wanna do that for? Far too many interesting things going on.' He cocked an eyebrow. 'I've been talking to Gandhi. Me and him, we're best mates now.'

'Mr Gandhi is a great man,' Ranjit said.

'Oh, he certainly is,' agreed the Doctor, and stretched, making his shoulders pop. Casually he asked, 'So you all set for today's little trip?'

Ranjit nodded determinedly. 'As long as you and Mr Gandhi are by my side, everything will be fine.' Then his expression changed, a frown crinkling his brow.

'Everything all right?' the Doctor asked.

'I promised my friend that I would meet him this morning. But with everything that has happened...' Ranjit's voice tailed off and he wafted a hand. 'It is no matter. It will be better this way. I'm sure my friend would not have proceeded without me.' He paused a moment.

The Doctor stayed silent, sensing that there was something else the boy wanted to say. Sure enough, a moment later, Ranjit asked, 'We will be... safe, won't we, Mr Doctor?'

The Doctor smiled and said airily, 'Yeah, course we will. Once you've faced one god of destruction you've faced 'em all.'

Ranjit looked reassured.

The Doctor said, 'So was this just a social call?'

The boy's eyes widened. 'Oh yes. I came to tell you that Mr Gopal is here with our transport. We can leave whenever you are ready.'

'Well, why didn't you say so in the first place?' said the Doctor, sweeping past Ranjit. 'Come on.'

A minute later he was looking up at the transport Gopal had provided, grinning all over his face.

'Elephants!' he exclaimed. 'You brought elephants!'

'Are they to your liking, Doctor?' asked Gopal anxiously.

The Doctor patted one of the elephants on its rough grey forehead, and it responded by raising its trunk and sniffing delicately at his hair.

'Oh yeah,' he said, 'brilliant. Better than a smelly old car any day.'

The four elephants had elaborate, multicoloured floral designs painted on their heads, trunks and ears. They wore bracelets of spherical bells on their feet, which jingled when they walked, and each was equipped with a howdah, a boxy, open-sided canopy edged with tassels, containing seating enough for two people.

Gopal looked pleased at the Doctor's approval. 'Where is Mr Gandhi?' he asked.

'In his shelter,' said the Doctor. 'I'll go and fetch him.'

He had taken no more than a couple of steps when a voice bellowed, 'Oi! Stay right there, buster.'

'Uh-oh, here comes trouble,' the Doctor murmured to Gopal, rolling his eyes. He spun round and opened his arms. 'Donna!'

One of the small, two-wheeled passenger vehicles known as tongas had come to a halt on the slight elevation of dusty road that ran alongside the camp. The wiry teenage boy who had been pulling the tonga lowered the handles carefully to the ground and offered a helping hand to its occupant.

Donna emerged a little ungracefully. She was wearing a plum-coloured dress of some silky material which shimmered in the sunlight, and a hat with a wide, floppy brim.

'Um… nice hat,' the Doctor said neutrally.

'I burn easily,' snapped Donna.

'You don't have to tell me,' muttered the Doctor. 'One flash of those eyes is enough to frazzle anyone.'

'What did you say?' Donna asked, picking her way down the dusty slope towards him.

'Nothing complimentary,' he said quickly, and then grinned again. 'Aw, but it's good to see you, looking all… purple and shiny. Come and give us a big hug.'

He ran towards her and threw his arms around her. She hugged him back for a moment, then realised what she was doing and shoved him away.

'No way. You're not getting round me like that. I'm annoyed with you.'

'What for?' he exclaimed, all shrill indignation.

'You were about to go swanning off without me.'

'No I wasn't.'

'Yes you were. You're off to some temple or other.'

He looked like a child caught with his hand in the sweetie jar. 'Who told you that?'

'Adelaide,' she said.

'Aw, you've met Adelaide? She's lovely, isn't she?'

'Doctor, don't try and sidetrack me.'

He saw the hurt look in her eyes and dropped the flippancy. 'Sorry,' he mumbled.

'Weren't you in the *least* bit concerned about me?' she asked.

'Course I was. That's why I came here. I was looking for you.'

'But you were still about to go off on one of your adventures.'

He opened his mouth as if to offer an excuse, then closed it again and sighed. 'I just got caught up in things. I was going to come and find you later. Promise. I knew you'd be all right.'

'How could you possibly know that?'

'Well, look at you. You're Donna. Tough as old...' he saw her face harden and said quickly '... resourceful and resilient. Blimey, you've even got a new wardrobe.' He punched her arm lightly. 'C'mon, don't be mad. Hey, I want you to meet someone.'

'Who?' she said as he grabbed her hand.

'It's a surprise, but I promise you're gonna love it. Come on.'

He led her through the camp, weaving between the shelters and lean-tos. Donna looked around, appalled at the poverty and suffering.

'Doctor, all these people—'

'Yeah, I know,' he said, centuries of sadness seemingly encapsulated in those three little words.

Eventually they came to a shabby lean-to, no

different from all the others. He nodded at the two young men sitting outside, then leaned towards the tatty sheets of cloth draped across its entrance. 'Knock, knock. You decent in there?'

There was an answering chuckle and a voice replied, 'Come in, Doctor.'

The Doctor lifted aside one of the sheets, said something to the occupant of the lean-to, and then turned to Donna, obviously relishing the moment.

'Donna Noble, may I introduce you to Mohandas Gandhi.'

Donna gave him an incredulous look, then stepped inside the shelter, which was dark and hot. A little old man wearing what looked like a white bed sheet was sitting cross-legged on a thin reed mat. He smiled almost toothlessly up at her.

'Hello, Donna Noble,' he said, pressing his palms together. 'I'm very pleased to meet you.'

'Likewise,' said Donna a little breathlessly. She was clearly overwhelmed. Then she blurted, 'Blimey, you look just like you do in the film.'

Gandhi looked at her quizzically. 'Film?'

'She means the newsreels,' said the Doctor quickly, stepping in front of her. 'I've just come to tell you that our transport is here, Mohandas. We're ready to roll whenever you are.'

Gandhi thanked him and said he would be there in a few minutes. As soon as they were out of earshot of the lean-to, Donna said, 'I can't believe it. Gandhi! The real Gandhi!'

The Doctor grinned delightedly at her enthusiasm. 'I know,' he said.

'Do all historical figures look just how you imagine?' she asked.

The Doctor pondered a moment. 'Well, not all of them. You know what they said about Cleopatra?'

'Most beautiful woman in the world, wasn't she?'

He clenched his teeth in a grimace.

'You mean that was all just hype?' said Donna.

'Well, let me put it this way – if the world had been the size of her bedchamber and all her handmaidens had had the day off, then there *might* have been a grain of truth in it.'

Donna laughed. Then she said, 'Hey, hang on. How do *you* know how big her bedchamber was?'

The Doctor sniffed and shot her a sidelong look. 'I've been around a bit, you know.'

She laughed harder and grabbed his hand. 'You old devil,' she said.

Cameron had a puncture. It had happened not long after he had set off, just as the sun was climbing a ladder of thinning purple clouds into a salmon-pink sky. He had fished his puncture-repair kit out of his knapsack and tried to mend it, but the heat had made the glue go runny and it wouldn't stick.

Eventually, hot and dirty, his fingers sticky with glue, he had given up. He had briefly considered turning back, and then had wondered whether it would be all right to leave his useless bike by the side of the road and continue on foot.

In the end he decided to carry on, but to wheel his bike along with him. He couldn't face turning back, and if he left his bike then someone would probably steal it.

Not that he had seen anyone, which was strange. True, it *was* still early morning, and the temple *was* situated off a quiet farming track out of the city, as opposed to a main route, which he had heard were populated by long caravans of people trying to escape the troubles. But even so, the wheat farmers and tea plantation workers were normally out in the fields by now, and whenever he and Ranjit had come this way before they had passed kids leading goats on strings, or the occasional camel-herder, or farmers riding rickety wooden carts pulled by skinny oxen.

Today, though, there was nobody, and Cameron could only guess that those who hadn't already fled were too scared by the fighting to stick their noses out of their front doors. He had heard Ronny and Father say that gangs of bandits had moved into the area and were using the violence as a smokescreen to rob and kill innocent people. Cameron wondered what *he* would do if a gang of bandits suddenly appeared on the road ahead of him. Would he hide, or run, or simply stand his ground and hope that because he was English, or a child, they would leave him alone?

All at once he glimpsed movement in the long grass at the side of the road about thirty metres ahead. Thinking it might be a bandit crawling along on his belly, getting ready to ambush him, he stopped. Then the 'bandit' revealed itself, and he saw it was not a bandit at all. It was a huge snake – at least six metres long and as thick as his thigh – and it came slithering out on to the road, leaving a winding track, like a series of Ss in the dust.

Cameron had seen snakes before, and he knew the thing to do was stand still and let them go about their business. In his eleven years in India, this advice had always stood him in good stead – but not today. To Cameron's horror the snake altered direction and began to slither towards him. When it was about fifteen metres away, it stopped, rearing up on its tail until it was taller than he was.

Though terrified, Cameron noticed a couple of things about the snake at once. Firstly, he noticed that its distinctive yellow and black markings, and its even more distinctive ability to flatten its upper ribs so that the area below its head flared out in a hood shape, identified it as a King Cobra. And secondly, he noticed that the creature was not only huge but oddly misshapen, its body bulging with the same strange black carbuncles that he had seen on the crocodile last night.

The Cobra regarded him with flat eyes, its head weaving from side to side. Its forked purple tongue flickered in and out of its mouth. Moving as slowly as he could, Cameron placed his rucksack on the ground and opened it. Suddenly the snake hissed, its head darting forward, its fangs dripping venom.

Cameron jumped back, heart pounding. He knew that a snake like this could kill him with a single bite. However, this was a feigned attack, a warning. The Cobra's head snapped back as though on a piece of elastic. Slowly Cameron reached into his rucksack and took out his catapult. Then he felt about on the ground until he found a suitable rock.

The Cobra lunged again, and again Cameron jumped back. He had no doubt that the snake would keep playing this game until it either killed him or he managed to drive it away. Mouth dry, he loaded his catapult with the rock, took careful aim and fired.

All his hours of practice paid off. The rock flew straight and true and struck the Cobra on its snout. It curled in on itself, dipping its head back into its nest of coils. Before it could recover, Cameron grabbed another rock, half-expecting the snake to come for him again.

But to his immense relief, the massive, misshapen Cobra had obviously decided it had had enough. It turned and slithered away, disappearing back into the long grass at the side of the road.

The Doctor and Donna were laughing their heads off.

Donna had started it. At first it had been the rolling motion of the elephants which had set her off, and then she had been suddenly struck by the wonderful absurdity of her situation, and after that there was no stopping her.

Gopal, Ranjit and the three men from Gandhi's entourage who had come along with them – quiet, studious types, very polite and diffident – had looked at her in astonishment, but the Doctor and Gandhi had seemed to understand. Gandhi smiled away, all avuncular good humour, and the Doctor, after grinning along for a bit, had become so caught up in the infectiousness of her mood that he had started to laugh too.

'Why do Mr Doctor and Miss Donna laugh so much?' Ranjit asked Gandhi, who he was riding with. 'Are they affected by the sun?'

Smiling, Gandhi said, 'No, they are affected by life. Sometimes a person feels its worth and joy so keenly that their only recourse is to express the emotion through laughter.'

'But aren't they scared of what awaits us in the temple?' Ranjit asked.

'No doubt they are. But sometimes fear of the danger

to come makes a person appreciate life all the more.'

It was the cry for help which finally snapped the Doctor and Donna out of it. As they approached a thickly wooded area of neem trees, they heard someone yell, 'Get away! Help! Heeeeelp!'

'That's a kid,' Donna said, but the Doctor had already leaped down from his elephant and was sprinting through the trees. He dodged between trunks and hurdled bushes, before bursting into a clearing. The abandoned temple loomed on the far side, but this wasn't what claimed his immediate attention.

Directly in front of him, standing with his back to the Doctor, was a boy holding a catapult. Closing in on the boy were at least thirty monkeys, all of which were hideously enlarged, their bodies made monstrous by zytron energy.

Clearly whatever was responsible for the leakage was close by. The physical symptoms were more advanced in these creatures than in the patients the Doctor had seen at the hospital. The monkeys were smothered in black lumps, some to such an extent that they could move only with extreme difficulty. They snarled and bared their teeth as they advanced; some were salivating like rabid dogs.

'Hello,' the Doctor said quietly to the boy. 'What's your name then?'

He had made plenty of noise crashing through the trees, but the boy's attention must have been focused on the threat in front of him. He spun round now with a shocked cry, firing his catapult instinctively. The Doctor ducked and the rock flew past his head and took a chunk out of a nearby tree.

'Whoa there, Dennis the Menace,' the Doctor said mildly. 'One thing I definitely don't need is a side parting.' He glanced at the monkeys, which were still edging forward. 'So what do they call you then?'

'Cameron Campbell,' replied the boy.

'Right then, Cameron Campbell, I want you to come over here and stand behind me. But do it slowly. Understand?'

Cameron nodded and did as the Doctor asked. A couple of the bigger monkeys hissed and scuttled forward, their twisted, lopsided movement making them look like giant injured spiders rather than primates.

The Doctor produced his sonic and clamped it between his teeth. Then he used both hands to delve into his jacket pockets. In a muffled voice he said, 'Now where did I put… aha!'

He produced a small, brightly coloured pyramid with a wick sticking out of the top. He spat his sonic back into his palm and used it to light the wick.

The pyramid fizzed and crackled, shooting out multicoloured sparks. Almost casually the Doctor tossed it into the middle of the advancing monkeys.

'I'd shut your eyes if I were you,' he told Cameron.

Suddenly there was a *fla-thoomp!* sound and ripples of multicoloured light radiated outwards from the fizzing pyramid. Screaming in alarm, the monkeys scattered in all directions, disappearing into the trees and bushes.

'And don't come back!' the Doctor shouted. 'There's more where that came from.' He looked down at Cameron. 'You can open your eyes now.'

Cameron did so, blinking up at him. Before he could speak there was a rustling noise behind them, and Donna, Gandhi, Gopal, Ranjit and one of Gandhi's attendants emerged from the bushes.

'We saw a light,' said Donna.

'Was it Shiva?' asked Ranjit fearfully.

'Nah, it was a Maluvian Rainbow Cascade. Fun for all the family,' said the Doctor.

Cameron saw Ranjit and his eyes widened. 'I waited for you!' he said. 'Why didn't you come?'

Ranjit looked shamefaced. 'I'm sorry. I met Bapu and told him what had happened. When he and Mr Doctor said they would come to the temple with me…' He shook his head 'I did not think you would come alone.'

'Well, you thought wrong,' said Cameron, scowling at his friend.

'Ah well, never mind, no harm done,' said the Doctor briskly. 'Right, I'm off for a quick nosey in the temple. Who's coming with me? Not you two.'

This last remark was directed at the boys. Ranjit looked relieved, but Cameron pulled a face.

'I haven't come all this way for nothing,' he protested.

'Yeah, you have. Sorry,' said the Doctor dismissively.

'I will take the boys back,' Gopal said. 'We will wait for you by the elephants.'

'Okey-dokey,' said the Doctor. 'See you in a bit.' He strode towards the temple's pillared entrance.

Donna hurried to catch up with him. 'You've got a way with kids,' she said heavily. 'You ought to be a teacher.'

'Been there, done that.' He took a reading of the building with his sonic.

'Anything?'

'Not sure.' He turned to Gandhi and his attendant, who were bringing up the rear. 'How you doing there, Mohandas?'

'I am ready for anything,' Gandhi said happily.

'Good man.'

They entered the temple, which felt refreshingly cool after the hot sun. It would have been gloomy had it not been for the bands of dusty light which spilled through the cracks in the ancient stonework.

'Doesn't seem to be anyone home,' she said.

'Certainly there is no sign of Shiva's light,' observed Gandhi.

'That's probably because the zytron engines of whatever landed here have powered down,' the Doctor speculated. 'But let's stay alert, people. Stick close to me. I'm the man with the plan.'

'And what plan's that then?' Donna asked.

The Doctor glanced at her and swallowed. 'Well, the plan to… um… have a quick look round and… see what's what.'

'Brilliant,' she said.

'Sometimes the simplest plans are the best ones,' he replied huffily.

They moved through the antechamber and into the shrine. Inside was a large open space with an altar at the far end. Aside from the archetypal Indian designs carved into the stonework, the layout wasn't all that different from the churches back home, Donna thought.

What seemed immediately clear to her was that the temple was empty and deserted, that whatever might have been here a week ago had now gone. She was about to say as much when she became aware of a strange silvery shimmer in the air. When the shimmer faded, a vast creature was standing in front of the altar.

She gasped, recognising the creature instantly. It was a massive, flame-red arachnid, from the front of which, rearing from the abdomen like a figurehead on a ship, was a vaguely humanoid female torso, encased in a ridged, armour-like exoskeleton. Instead of hands the 'spider-woman' had lethal-looking spikes, and her parody of a human face was set in a grinning snarl, the slavering mouth filled with jagged teeth, the eyes black and staring. There were more eyes, a whole row of them, on the crown-like crest that jutted above the spider-woman's brow.

Donna clutched the Doctor's arm, her legs turning to water. 'Oh my God, Doctor, it's the Racnoss,' she said.

The Doctor looked at her curiously, but said nothing. On the other side of him, Gandhi's attendant had fallen to his knees and bowed his head. 'Shiva, forgive me, Shiva, forgive me,' he muttered over and over again.

Gandhi was standing at the Doctor's shoulder, staring up as though mesmerised.

'What do you see, Mohandas?' the Doctor asked quietly.

'I see a great darkness, Doctor,' Gandhi said, trying to keep his voice steady. 'A great darkness descending on the world.'

The Doctor nodded grimly and held up his sonic. 'Well, all I see is a door that needs opening. Cover your ears.'

The sonic began to shriek, its blue tip glowing so brightly it was almost white.

Donna saw the Empress of the Racnoss flicker and distort, like a bad TV picture. Then the massive creature shattered into a million silvery fragments, which seemed to be instantly sucked into a central point, like dust into the nozzle of a powerful vacuum cleaner. A second later there was no evidence that the Racnoss had ever been there. The temple was empty and silent once more.

FIVE

The central flight deck of the alien craft resembled a cave of smooth black rock, filled with a glowing plastic web interlaced with silvery-black lumps of metal. Pulsing strands and filaments snaked everywhere – some lashed together in knotted clumps; some trailing across the ridged floor like jungle vines; some hanging in fleshy loops from the uneven walls and ceiling. The metallic elements fused into the web most closely resembled machines, or bits of machines, that had melted and reformed many times over. They were studded with spines and nodules that glittered and flickered with intermittent ripples of milky light.

The impression was that of an amateurish botch-job, a tangled lash-up of random elements that couldn't possibly work. And yet it *did* work, the craft's intricately interwoven systems united by one crucial component. That component, ensconced in its messy cradle of technology, like a hospital patient hooked up to a dozen life-support machines, was the alien which had piloted the ship to Earth.

Right now the alien was agitated, having been caught unawares by the sonic attack. Its scans had revealed the inhabitants of this planet to be a level 2 species, yet the sonic attack had been consistent with a level 6 civilisation. If it hadn't been for the presence of its quarry, the pilot might not even have bothered setting the sensors which were linked to the displacement system. Fortunately, the sensors had interpreted the sonic attack as a hostile action and had automatically issued a relocation directive.

But the source of the sonic device still bothered the pilot. It didn't think its quarry possessed such an instrument – unless it had stolen technology far in advance of its own. If so, then its quarry could prove more dangerous than had been anticipated. The pilot decided that steps would have to be taken if it didn't want to be caught out a second time.

It sent out a thought-pulse to initiate a level 6 technology scan, and received the results within seconds. Negative. Which meant that the sonic device was now inactive. It sent out another pulse, priming the scanners to detect any re-occurrence of sonic energy waves.

Now if the sonic device was activated again it would be ready.

'So what *was* that thing in the temple?' Donna asked.

They were sitting on the elephants again, heading back to camp. Since the Racnoss had disappeared, the Doctor had been deep in thought, responding to her questions with little more than grunts. She had been patient up to now, but if he didn't give her some proper answers soon she'd explode.

He blinked at her, as if roused from sleep. 'It was a glamour,' he said.

'And what's one of those when it's at home?'

'It's a...' He glanced at Gandhi, his attendants, Gopal and the two boys, all of whom were looking at him with interest. He pulled a face, knowing this wasn't going to be easy, and then sighed, deciding as ever that the best policy was to plough on regardless.

'It's a kind of psychic shield,' he said. 'It was developed by the Kladdavoreesh to protect themselves from the squillions of predators on their planet.' He grimaced. 'Nasty planet, Kladdavor. Once got invited to a feasting ceremony just outside the Toxic Zone. Never again. Anyway, once word got about, glamour technology was copied, developed and adapted by loads of different species, often for military use or criminal gain.'

'And it... what? Makes you see what you're most

scared of?'

'In this case, yeah. The intention being that instead of hanging around you run very fast in the opposite direction.'

'So you can't tell, just from looking at this glamour thingy, who's using it?' Donna asked.

'No, could be any one of... ooh, seventy-three thousand, nine hundred and twenty-four different species, give or take.'

'And how come it disappeared when you zapped it?'

'Must have had an in-built displacement system, which means that whenever anyone mucks about with it, it alerts the craft it's shielding, which then hops off somewhere else.'

'Could do with one of them for my car,' said Donna. She looked round at Gandhi, who was sitting cross-legged on the elephant behind them, listening to their exchange with interest. 'Sorry about this, Mr Gandhi,' she said. 'We must sound like total nutters to you.'

'On the contrary,' said Gandhi, 'your conversation is fascinating.'

'You mean you believe all this alien planet stuff? Just like that?' She indicated the Doctor. 'First time I met him, I thought he'd escaped from somewhere.'

Gandhi's eyes sparkled with interest and intelligence. He might be an old bloke, Donna thought, but even in the short time she'd known him she'd decided he was one of the sharpest people she'd ever met. Like the Doctor, he gave the impression that nothing got past him, that he could adapt to any situation.

'You have no reason to lie to me,' he said, 'and how can I do anything but accept the evidence of my own eyes?'

'But none of this… bothers you?' Donna said. 'I know tons of people who'd shut themselves in the wardrobe if they found out all this stuff was real.'

Gandhi smiled his near-toothless smile. 'Forgive my impertinence, Donna, but I believe this highlights the cultural difference between the East and the West. You see, the bridges of the West are made of concrete and steel and wire, whereas the bridges of the East are made of spirit. To communicate in the West you move and talk, and everything must have a definite resolution, but in the East we sit and contemplate and suffer and dream. There are no boundaries for us. Everything remains possible.'

Donna looked at him in admiration. 'That's… brilliant,' she said. 'Yeah, I totally get that. I've never thought of it like that before.'

Perched on his elephant, the Doctor grinned. 'That's Mohandas for you,' he said. 'The soul of an Eastern prophet and the spirit of a Galactic pioneer.'

Gandhi placed his palms together and gave a little bow. 'You are too kind, Doctor.'

'Nah, not me,' said the Doctor. 'Doesn't pay to be too

kind. Always be just kind enough and you won't go far wrong.'

By the time they arrived back at the camp, the sun was high in the sky. Donna was glad to get her feet on solid ground again. The continuous motion had made her feel sick, and even with the umbrella to keep off the worst of the sun it had been getting very hot and a bit smelly.

'Right,' the Doctor said, jumping down from his elephant, 'onwards and upwards. Gopal, Mohandas, see you later. If you hear news of Shiva, or any other deity, popping up in any nearby temples, give us a shout. Donna, seeing as the Campbells are mates of yours, will you take Cameron home? I'll join you there in a bit.'

He turned away, but Donna said, 'Hang on, where are *you* going?'

'Back to the TARDIS. I want to scan the area for hotspots of zytron energy, see if I can find out where that ship's gone.'

He turned away again. Donna asked, 'What *is* zytron energy anyway?'

He turned back, sighed. 'It's appallingly dangerous is what it is. It's cheap and adaptable, but unstable and hard to contain. It attacks, mutates and eventually destroys living tissue. Put bluntly, it turns whoever and whatever it infects into a ravening psychopathic monster.'

Donna pulled a face. 'You'd better go and sort it then. See you later, spaceman.' Before the Doctor could turn away for the third time, she said sternly, 'But don't go getting into any trouble without me, OK?'

'As if,' said the Doctor innocently.

'You spoil that boy,' Sir Edgar grunted as his wife left the dining room with a tray of boiled eggs and hot buttered toast. Two minutes later her panicked cries brought everyone running.

'What is it, Mother?' asked Adelaide.

'It's Cameron. He's gone,' Mary replied in a weak voice, and promptly swooned in her arms.

Ten minutes later, after a thorough search of the house and grounds, it was confirmed that Cameron was nowhere to be found.

'He's been kidnapped, I know he has,' said Mary, who was now lying on the chaise-longue in the drawing room, looking white and ill.

'Nonsense,' said Sir Edgar, though he too looked anxious.

Ronny appeared, having given the grounds another onceover. 'His bicycle's missing from the shed,' he told them.

'There you are,' said Adelaide, trying to remain positive. 'He's probably gone off on one of his expeditions.'

At that moment, there came an explosive

hammering on the front door. They all looked at each other, frightened by the urgency of the sound, but unwilling to speculate what it might mean. For a few moments they stood in silence, waiting. Eventually there was a tap on the drawing room door and Becharji entered.

'Major Daker is here, sahib,' he said to Sir Edgar.

Sir Edgar glanced at Ronny. 'What does he want?'

'He says that he needs to speak to you, sahib. Urgently.'

'Better show him in then,' said Sir Edgar.

Seconds later Major Daker clomped into the room. He looked even more red-faced than usual – and, Adelaide noted, unusually dishevelled. He glanced round as if surprised to see them all there, and then turned his attention to Sir Edgar.

'Begging your pardon, Sir Edgar, but I need to speak to you at once.'

'Is it about Cameron?' Adelaide blurted.

Daker blinked at her, surprised. 'Cameron? No, why? What's he done?'

'He's gone missing,' she said.

Daker stared at her for so long that she felt unsettled. She noticed how bloodshot his eyes were, the whites almost pink.

'Sedition,' he muttered eventually.

'I beg your pardon?' said Ronny.

Daker swung round on him. 'Don't you see? They

want us out and this is their way of trying to force our hand.'

Ronny and Adelaide looked at each other, baffled. 'Who do?' Ronny asked.

'The natives, of course. The *Indians*. I came to tell you that three of my men disappeared last night. Taken from their beds two of them, right under the noses of their colleagues.' His eyes clouded over, as if he had lost his thread, and he rubbed vigorously at what Adelaide noticed was a darkish lump behind his left ear. Then he said, 'It's all very well these people fighting amongst themselves, but I tell you, they've overstepped the mark this time.'

A little unnerved, Adelaide said, 'I'm sure Cameron's not been taken by anyone. He's been so cooped up recently, what with—'

But, with a terse shake of the head, Daker cut her off. 'We have to come down hard on these people, show them who's boss.' He snapped suddenly to attention. Adelaide almost expected him to salute. 'With your permission, Sir Edgar, I would like to instigate a thorough search of the city. It is my intention to leave no stone unturned.'

Sir Edgar wafted a hand, too anxious about his son to put up with the Major's bluster.

'Do whatever you think fit, Major Daker,' he said. 'I trust you'll let us know the instant you hear anything of Cameron's whereabouts?'

'You have my word, sir,' Daker said, and this time he *did* salute.

He turned and exited the room, rubbing at the lump behind his ear.

The Doctor was a blur of movement, leaping around the TARDIS console, flicking switches and spinning dials. When the locational calibrator stuck, he whacked it with a rubber mallet and it burped into life, like an old man shocked out of an afternoon nap. Every five seconds, he checked the scanner screen, across which a complicated mass of data was scrolling. 'Come on, come on, get to the point,' he said as his eyes flickered across the numbers and symbols. Finally, after another few madcap circuits of the console, he shouted, 'Aha! There you go, you beauty!'

He delved into his jacket. Now all he had to do was pinpoint the exact location by configuring the data with the old sonic and…

Suddenly he frowned. The sonic wasn't there. He tried the other pocket. Not there either. Frantically he patted each of his pockets in turn, then turned them out, scattering plum stones, a rubber spider, scribbled notes, a book, a tangle of green and yellow wire, sweet wrappers, a yo-yo and all sorts of alien bits and bobs across the floor.

'No, no, no, no, no, no, no!' he shouted, trying to remember when he had last used the sonic, and more importantly where he had put it afterwards.

It had been in the temple. He'd used it on the glamour. And then, and then…

He slapped himself so hard on the side of the head that it sounded like the crack of a whip.

'Idiot!' he yelled.

SIX

'Hey!' shouted Ranjit, then wished he'd kept his mouth shut. The little kid was still some distance away, and as soon as he saw Ranjit coming, he ran.

It had been the sunlight flashing off its shiny surface which had caught Ranjit's attention. He had turned to see the little kid showing off the Doctor's magic torch to a group of his friends. The kid was waving the torch in the air, and all the other kids were oohing and aahing.

Straight away Ranjit realised that the torch must have flown out of the Doctor's pocket when he had jumped down from the elephant.

Maybe the kid had seen it fly out, or maybe he had found it later in the dust. Either way, Ranjit knew that the magic torch was a very precious piece of equipment and that the Doctor would want it back.

The kid was running now, up the dusty banking onto the road, then towards the field beyond. The kid was younger than Ranjit, maybe seven or eight, but he had a good lead and the grass in the field was long enough for him to hide in.

Ranjit gave chase, his bare feet slapping the sun-baked earth, sending up a trail of dust. People turned to watch him as he pounded by, but no one challenged him or tried to stop him. He reached the top of the rise just in time to see the kid plunge into the high grass on the other side of the road. The grass came up to the kid's neck. All Ranjit could see of him now was his head bobbing up and down, like a ball floating on a green sea.

Ranjit knew he would catch the kid eventually, but his fear was that the kid would panic and throw the torch away. If he did, they might never find it in the long grass.

With this in mind, he halted on the edge of the field and cupped his hands around his mouth.

'Stop!' he shouted. 'I only want to talk to you!'

But the kid didn't stop. If anything, he ran faster. Ranjit sighed and went after him. It was not easy running in the long grass. The sun had dried it out, making it hard and spiky. It scratched his legs, drawing stripes of blood here and there. Ranjit knew that the field was probably full of creatures that could bite and sting: snakes, spiders, scorpions. If one of them bit him, he might think it was just the grass scratching him. Venom might race around his body without him even knowing it.

And if that happened, who would help him? Who would see him if he collapsed in the long grass? His Uncle Mahmoud's next-door neighbour had been stung by a scorpion once, a big one. Uncle Mahmoud had sucked out the poison. He had told Ranjit that it tasted like goat's milk, but Ranjit hadn't believed him.

He was gaining on the kid now. The kid was halfway across the field, Ranjit only thirty or forty metres behind. Ranjit's head throbbed where the rock had hit him, but otherwise he felt pretty good. On the way to the temple that morning, Bapu had shared his breakfast with him – bread, oranges, grapes, sour lemons and strained butter with a juice of aloe – and so for the first time in days his belly felt full and his limbs strong.

All at once, the kid spun round, pointing the magic torch at Ranjit.

'Leave me alone or I'll shoot you!'

Ranjit stopped, his legs stinging, sweat trickling down his face. He laughed. 'That's not a gun.'

The kid was thin, with dark hollows under his eyes. He turned the torch on. It glowed blue and made a high-pitched noise, but nothing else happened.

'You see,' said Ranjit. He held out his hand. 'Now give it to me.'

The kid shook his head. 'It's not yours.'

'It's not yours either. You stole it.'

'I didn't steal it,' said the kid indignantly. 'I found it. The Englishman dropped it.'

'If you saw him drop it, why didn't you give it back to him?'

The kid looked flustered for a moment. Then he said, 'I was going to. I hoped he might give me a reward for it, so that I could buy food for my family.'

Ranjit shook his head. 'Just because you're hungry, that doesn't mean you should become a thief. Mr Doctor is a good man. He's trying to help us.'

'I'm not a thief,' protested the kid. 'Is it my fault if the Englishman is careless?'

Ranjit held out his hand again. 'Give me the torch. I'll give it back to Mr Doctor. I'll tell him that you found it. Maybe he'll give you a reward and maybe he won't.'

But the kid shook his head and tightened his grip on the torch. 'I won't give it back.'

'Yes you will,' said Ranjit, stepping towards him.

The kid turned to run and Ranjit jumped on him, wrestling him to the ground. For a few seconds, the two boys fought furiously. Ranjit tried to grab the torch, but the kid held on to it for dear life. The younger boy's thumb pressed down on a row of tiny controls on the side of the instrument and it began to shriek as though in pain, its tip glowing a brilliant white-blue.

***

There! This time the readings came through loud and clear. Not only had the scanners detected the sonic energy waves of the level 6 device, but they had now been able to pinpoint its location. Assimilating the information, the alien pilot sent out a thought-pulse.

Ranjit finally succeeded in wrenching the torch out of the kid's hand. However, he pulled so violently that the torch flew end over end, describing an arc in the air.

Ranjit sat up, grass poking out of his hair and sticking to his sweaty skin. He jumped to his feet just in time to register roughly where it had landed. He waded through the grass, trying to keep his eye on the spot.

Though the kid had fought hard to keep hold of the torch, he had now given up on it. He sat in the middle of the crushed patch of grass where he and Ranjit had been wrestling, arms folded and mouth down-turned in a sulk.

Ranjit poked about in the long grass where he had seen the torch land, tearing clumps of it out in frustration. At last he saw a whitish glimmer and snatched it up. He straightened just in time to see a strange silvery shimmer in the air.

Next moment, two men were standing in the long grass about twenty metres away. Their skin was white, like chalk, but it was their faces which almost stopped the breath in his throat. They had no eyes; just smooth, pale hollows of unbroken flesh. They neither smiled nor spoke nor showed any emotion at all. They simply began striding, fluidly and remorselessly, in Ranjit's direction.

Ranjit had never been so terrified. There was something awful about these men. He turned and ran, his fear making him stumble, his breath hitching raggedly in his throat.

The kid was still sitting where Ranjit had left him, arms folded. Ranjit realised the kid couldn't see the terrible men above the long grass.

'Run!' he shouted, his voice raw and high-pitched. 'Run now!'

The kid just scowled at him, stuck out his bottom lip and turned away.

Ranjit could see the men coming towards him out of the corner of his eye. He hated leaving the kid, but he didn't have time to argue. If he paused for even two more seconds, the men would get them both. And so, feeling sick, he ran past the kid, deeper into the field, towards the tall trees on the far side.

He was halfway between the kid and the trees when he heard the kid scream. It was a hot day, but the sound was so full of terror that it made Ranjit feel cold all over.

Ranjit looked back and saw the kid trying to scramble to his feet as the men loomed over him. He managed it, but as he turned to run the men reached out and grabbed him with their awful white hands.

'No!' Ranjit shouted, but then there was another silvery shimmer. When his eyes cleared a moment later, Ranjit realised he was shouting at nothing. The two men and the kid were gone.

SEVEN

'Don't you ever get the urge to do something...
y'know... *naughty*?' Donna said.

Gandhi chuckled. 'Naughty?'

'Yeah, don't you ever just wanna have a day off
from helping other people, and... I dunno... go on a
shopping spree or... just bask in the sun and pig out
on chocolate?'

Gandhi was laughing now. He clapped his hands in
delight. 'I *do* like chocolate,' he admitted.

'Well, there you go then.'

'But I deny myself the pleasure of it.'

'But *why*?' Donna asked. 'I mean, look at all the
fantastic things you do for people. Surely you, more
than anyone, deserve a treat now and again?'

They were sitting in a tonga, heading back towards

the Campbells' palatial property on the outskirts of the most salubrious area of Calcutta. Cameron was perched between Donna and Gandhi, his bicycle strapped to the back of the little carriage.

Gandhi had an appointment with Sir Edgar to discuss possible solutions to the recent troubles, and had asked if he could tag along. Donna had been delighted. She had already grown fond of the little man. His selfless good humour, open-mindedness and *joie de vivre* made her think of an older version of the Doctor.

'Have you heard of *The Gita*, Donna?' he asked now.

She frowned, vaguely recalling a drunken pub conversation she had once had with Amrita, a work colleague at H.C. Clements, before all the Racnoss business had kicked off.

'It's a holy book, innit? Krishna and all that?'

Gandhi nodded. 'A passage in *The Gita* describes the ideal man. He is desireless. His aim is to reach the highest state of perfection, to transcend his physical being and become one with God – to achieve Nirvana.'

'And that's what you're trying to do, is it?'

Gandhi inclined his head. 'It is a daily struggle.'

'Well, good luck to you,' Donna said. 'If anyone can get there, it's you. Me, I'd have no chance. One whiff of a Cadbury's Wispa and I'd slip right off that pedestal.'

As the tonga came to a halt outside the imposing black gates of the Campbells' house, Cameron shrank back into his seat.

'Time to face the music, mate,' Donna said not unkindly.

'I'm going to be in so much trouble,' whimpered Cameron.

She pulled a sympathetic face. 'Might not be as bad as you think. I mean, they're hardly gonna bawl you out with His Lordship in the house, are they?' She flipped a thumb at Gandhi, who was being helped out of the carriage by a reverential tonga-wallah. 'It'll be all "how do you do?", best china and cucumber sandwiches. It'll have blown over by teatime.'

The look on Becharji's austere face when he opened the door was priceless. Donna had never seen a man do so many goggle-eyed double-takes before. She had to bite her bottom lip to stop herself laughing out loud.

'Me again,' she said eventually. 'And this time I've brought a couple of mates along.'

Becharji looked at her with a glazed expression, and then with a little shake of the head he recovered his composure.

'Of course. Um… please come in. I'll inform Sir Edgar that you're here.'

They stepped onto the polished wooden floor of the elegant hallway as Becharji hurried away. An aspidistra bloomed in a large ceramic pot in the corner by the door; a ceiling fan rotated elegantly overhead.

'Wait for it,' said Donna.

No sooner were the words out of her mouth than

the door to the parlour flew open and Mary Campbell emerged, wet-eyed and red-nosed. She saw Cameron and gave a little scream.

She was dashing forward, long-limbed and awkward, pearls swinging around her neck, when she registered Gandhi, standing there in his homespun robe. She faltered, torn between an unseemly display of emotion and the decorum she knew she ought to show in such circumstances.

In the end, it was Cameron who rushed forward, arms outstretched. 'I'm sorry, Mother,' he cried, and promptly burst into tears.

Mary hugged her son. 'It's all right, darling. You're home safely. That's all that matters.'

Next to emerge was Adelaide, red-cheeked and beaming with relief. She strode forward and ruffled her younger brother's hair. 'Where have you been, you little scamp?' she said affectionately.

Just behind her was Ronny, who half-heartedly scolded Cameron for worrying them all to death. Adelaide smiled at Gandhi, palms pressed together in the traditional Hindu greeting.

'Mr Gandhi, welcome,' she said. 'How lovely to see you again.' She turned to Donna and took her hands. 'And Donna. What brings you back here so soon?'

'Oh, you know,' said Donna, nodding at Gandhi, 'someone had to keep an eye on these two.'

A flurry of greetings and questions and gabbled

explanations followed. Sir Edgar huffed and blustered, apologising to Gandhi and stooping to mutter to Cameron that he would have words with him later. Finally he suggested that he and Gandhi retreat to the study, leaving everyone else to take tea in the parlour.

'I'll just use the telephone in the study, if I may?' Ronny said.

Sir Edgar looked exasperated. 'Whatever for?'

'Thought I'd better let old Daker know that Cameron is safe before he turns Calcutta upside down.'

He hurried away, but was back a few minutes later. 'Too late, I'm afraid. Daker's already left.'

Sir Edgar raised an eyebrow. 'No doubt he'll be giving the locals what for by now,' he said, unable to hide the approval in his voice.

Donna looked at him with a flinty expression. 'And you think that's good, do you?' she said curtly.

Ronny and Adelaide exchanged a look, then Ronny stepped smartly forward, taking Donna's arm and steering her away from his father.

'Tea, Donna?' he said, clenching his teeth in a desperate grin.

The streets were narrow and dirty, the cramped dwellings shabby and run down, patched up with planks of wood and rusty sheets of corrugated iron. Daker and his troops were moving in groups through the poorest areas of Calcutta, from street to street and door to door, searching for what the Major described as 'insurgents', enemies of the state.

Private Wilkins and four of his colleagues were in the Major's group, and Wilkins for one was feeling uneasy. As the morning had worn on, and no clue had been found to the whereabouts of the three missing soldiers, Major Daker had started to become increasingly angry, increasingly unreasonable and increasingly… well, *unstable* was not too strong a word in Wilkins' opinion.

He watched as the Major strode forward and hammered on yet another door. Many of the buildings they had tried had been abandoned, left to the rats and cockroaches. This infuriated the Major. He seemed to think that if a family had fled, it was because they had something to hide rather than because they were frightened of becoming victims of the almost-nightly violence.

Major Daker used the butt of his revolver to bash on the door, leaving dents in the wood. 'Open up!' he barked. 'This is the British Army.'

After a moment the door opened a crack and a young Indian man peered out, clearly frightened.

'What took you so long?' Daker demanded. 'What are you hiding in there?'

The Indian man shook his head. In broken English he said, 'Please… this is my house… nothing here for you.'

'I'll be the judge of that,' Daker said. 'Stand aside.'

He stepped forward, shoving at the door. The man tried to resist, but Daker was too strong for him. The man staggered back as the door flew open.

Daker strode in, brandishing his revolver.

The building was little more than a dingy hovel. The place smelled musty and closed in. There was sacking on the floor and condensation ran down the walls.

A woman and three small children were huddled in one corner, the woman gathering the children to her. She was clearly terrified of the soldiers.

Stepping into the house behind the Major, Wilkins saw the children staring at him with big round eyes and tried to smile reassuringly.

Daker looked around, contempt on his face. 'An English boy and three soldiers have gone missing,' he said. 'I don't suppose you'd know anything about that, eh?'

The Indian man shook his head vigorously. 'No, sahib. We know nothing.'

'What's through there?' Daker jabbed his revolver towards an arch in the back wall, across which was hung a grubby piece of material.

The Indian man mimed resting his head on his hands. 'We sleep… yes?' he tried to explain.

'The bedroom?' Wilkins said, trying to help him out. 'Beds?'

'Beds, yes.'

Daker turned to one of the men. 'Check it out, Barnes.'

'Yessir.'

Barnes stomped across the room and yanked aside the sheet of material so violently that it fell off the wall. One of the children burst into tears.

'Please, sahib,' the man protested, raising his hands. 'You frighten my...' he gestured towards his wife and children. 'We know nothing, yes?'

Daker's eyes were glinting dangerously beneath the brim of his peaked cap. Wilkins noticed that he was swaying slightly from side to side.

'You're a liar,' he muttered. Then suddenly he started to shout, making the other children cry too. '*You people are all the same. All liars!*'

Wilkins glanced at his colleagues. They looked back at him, shaking their heads.

Barnes emerged from the arch. 'Nothing there, sir.'

A glazed look had come over Daker's face. He turned his head stiffly in the Indian man's direction.

'Where are they?' he said.

'Please...' The Indian man glanced at Wilkins, as if begging him for support.

Daker took a step forward, raising his revolver.

His voice was horribly low and silky, but it could still be heard above the crying of the children. 'Tell me where they are.'

Wilkins swallowed and stepped forward.

'Sir,' he said.

Daker appeared not to hear him.

Wilkins raised his voice. 'Sir, I don't think these people know anything.'

Daker stopped dead. He stood swaying for a moment, and then he slowly turned to face Wilkins.

'What?' he said quietly.

Wilkins felt sweat running down his face. 'I really don't think these people know anything, sir.'

Daker's face suddenly twisted. 'Are you siding with the enemy, Wilkins?' he snarled.

'They're not the enemy, sir,' said Wilkins. 'They're just a poor family, trying to get by in difficult times.'

'Traitor!' screamed Daker.

He lunged forward, and suddenly shoved Wilkins out of the door.

Wilkins staggered backwards into the street. Blinded by the sun, he toppled over, landing on his back in the dust. He lay for a moment, winded, and then tried to rise.

All at once a dark shape loomed over him, blotting out the sun. Shielding his eyes, Wilkins saw Major Daker pointing a revolver at his head.

Staring into the circular black barrel of the gun, Wilkins wondered whether he would hear the explosion of the discharged bullet in the split-second before it ended his life.

***

The Doctor emerged from the TARDIS, holding his timey-wimey detector. It looked as if it had been cobbled together from an alarm clock, a steam iron, an old Bakelite telephone and a reel-to-reel tape recorder. It hummed and clicked as he waved it in a wide arc in front of him.

'Hnn,' he grunted, clearly unimpressed. He made some minor adjustments to a row of rotating wheels of numbers that looked as if they had been cannibalised from an old adding machine, then held the device up again.

This time the detector began to ping in a steady, high-pitched rhythm. A grin spread across the Doctor's face.

'Captain Kangaroo, we have lift-off!' he shouted to no one in particular, and ran off up the street.

Wilkins tried to remain calm. He forced his attention away from the barrel of the revolver and up to the flushed face of his commanding officer. Major Daker's peaked cap plunged the top half of his face into shadow, so Wilkins concentrated on his mouth – his lips stretched tight over clenched teeth gleaming with spittle.

'You're not going to shoot me, are you, sir?' Wilkins asked, amazed at the steadiness of his voice.

He saw the Major's lips writhe. 'Why not? At El Alamein we executed traitors and cowards.'

'But I'm neither, sir,' said Wilkins. 'I was only offering an opinion.'

'*Insubordination!*' Daker screeched. 'You were questioning my orders.'

'You didn't actually *give* any orders, sir,' said a voice from behind Daker.

He whirled round. '*What?*'

The speaker was a blond, fresh-faced private called Joe Shaw. He looked terrified, but he cleared his throat and said, 'You didn't actually give any orders. Like Wilkins said, sir, he was just offering an opinion.' He hesitated a moment, then swallowed. 'And to be fair, sir, I agree with him… Wilkins, that is. I don't think the family know anything either.'

There were mumbles of agreement from the rest of the men, all of whom had now gathered in the street.

Daker looked furious. He swung from one to the other, waving his revolver about, pointing it at each of them in turn.

'*This is outrageous!*' he screamed. '*I'll shoot the damn lot of you!*'

'What for, sir?' asked Barnes.

'*For questioning my authority!*' Daker screamed, froth flying from his mouth.

'But you can't shoot us for that, sir,' Wilkins said from his sitting position. Oddly, as his superior officer lost control, the more *in* control he felt. 'You could put us on a charge, sir. Even court martial us. But you can't *shoot* us, sir. That would be…'

'Murder,' said Joe Shaw.

The rest of the men nodded.

Daker looked like a cornered animal, his eyes bulging in the crescent of shadow beneath his cap. He was still clutching his revolver, and suddenly Wilkins saw his knuckles whiten as his fingers tightened on the trigger.

'Look out!' he shouted, and the four standing men dived for cover, two to the left, two to the right. Just as his finger pulled the trigger, Daker jerked the gun up and the bullet went high, hitting the upper storey of a building across the road, sending stone splinters flying in all directions.

Wilkins wondered whether he should try jumping the Major, wrestling the gun out of his grasp, but there was no need. As though pulling the trigger had released all his pent-up fury, Daker suddenly allowed the revolver to slip from his nerveless fingers. A moment later he crumpled, dropping forward on to his knees and then slumping back on to his haunches. His men looked at each other, shocked, as he began to wail like a baby.

Wilkins stood up, not sure what to do or say. 'Sir,' he said hesitantly, 'I…'

But then Daker's hands rose and began scrabbling at his head, dislodging his cap.

Immediately the men jumped back, their shocked

expressions changing to horrified gasps.

As Daker's cap dropped into the dust, they all stared at the bulging black growths sprouting from his skull like gnarled and poisonous toadstools.

EIGHT

The readings on the timey-wimey detector kept changing. Like someone having to constantly retune a car radio whilst passing through an area of bad reception, the Doctor had to stop and twiddle dials every couple of minutes to keep the pinging noise constant.

He knew what this meant. The sonic was on the move. Clearly it was in somebody's possession and they were carrying it about with them. He had configured the detector to home in on the residual artron energy from the Time Vortex that would be clinging to the sonic. Genius that he was, he had instructed the machine to phase out the larger concentrations of energy that he and Donna would be carrying about with them and to focus on the smaller stuff. Of course, the detector might ping excitedly away, only for the Doctor to discover it had tracked down his lost sun visor or Donna's sandals. But sooner or later it would find the sonic. It was just a matter of... well, time.

At the moment the detector was pinging away like billy-o. The Doctor ran down street after street in pursuit of the signal. He was only peripherally aware of his surroundings, hardly conscious of the curious stares he was receiving from locals braving the riot-torn but currently quiet streets, and British soldiers on foot patrol, alert for signs of trouble.

As far as the Doctor was concerned, they could stare all they liked just as long as they left him alone. He had entered the Intergalactic Staring Championships once on Acerlago Prime and was used to being gawped at. He had come away with bronze, but only because the Rallion Gestalt had cheated. He was remembering what a fuss he had kicked up at the time, and how such things had seemed important to him back then, when he rounded a corner and ran slap-bang into someone.

He bounced off, rubbing his nose. The man he had collided with was at least two metres tall and seemed almost as wide. Like many of the local men, he was wearing a white cotton kurta over a pair of salwar pants. He had a bushy black beard and a tangled mass of black hair.

'Oof, sorry,' said the Doctor, and then he got his first *proper* look at the man. He saw how the man's body had ballooned and twisted with zytron energy, how his face had swollen and blackened, how the pigment had seeped out of his eyes, so that they now looked as yellow as a cat's.

He saw too that the man was wielding a club which was thicker and longer than his own leg. A club which he was now raising into the air with the clear intention of smashing it down on the Doctor's head.

The man roared and brought the club down in a savage arc. If the Doctor hadn't leaped backwards, the blow would have shattered his skull. He saved himself, but was unable to save the timey-wimey detector. It was smashed out of his hand, bits of it flying in all directions. However, it didn't actually stop pinging until it hit the ground and broke in two.

'Oh,' said the Doctor, looking down at the machine. 'That was a bit—' Then he threw himself backwards as the man swung the club again. The end swished past the Doctor's face, so close that he felt the breeze of it ruffle his hair.

'Whoa there, big feller,' he said, raising his hands. He wondered whether a Venusian lullaby might help. He had quite a repertoire of those.

The man snarled, drool spilling from his lips, and came for him again. Once more the Doctor ducked, and once more the club narrowly missed his head.

'You don't have to do this,' the Doctor said urgently, backing away. 'You're ill, but you can fight it – and I can help you. Because you're not a violent man, are you? I bet you go all gooey at the sight of babies and small fluffy animals. I'm right, aren't I? Cos underneath all that hair, I can see you've got a really kind—'

The man roared and charged. As he raised the club for another almighty swing, the Doctor's heel came down on a loose bit of debris – a rock or a chunk of wood – which flew out from under him. His left leg jerked into the air, and suddenly he found himself sprawling on his back in the dust. He was looking into his assailant's yellow eyes as the man raised the club to deliver the killing blow, when a shot rang out.

Instantly the man's hands opened, releasing the club. It fell to the ground, landing on its end before toppling over like a felled tree. A second later, the man collapsed too, legs crumpling as he fell forward. He would have fallen right on top of the Doctor if the Doctor hadn't rolled aside.

Springing to his feet, the Doctor saw a young British soldier running towards him, carrying a rifle. The soldier looked down at the bearded man as though appalled at what he had done. 'Are you all right, sir?' he asked.

The Doctor slapped dust from his blue suit. Furiously he said, 'What did you shoot him for?'

The young soldier quailed. 'He… he was attacking you, sir. He might have killed you. I shouted for him to stop, but he ignored me.'

'He's sick,' retorted the Doctor. 'Can't you see he's sick? Isn't it *obvious*?'

Stricken and pale, the young soldier shook his head. 'Sorry, sir, I... I didn't know.'

The Doctor glared at the soldier for a few more seconds, then his expression softened. 'No,' he said, 'I don't suppose you did.' He squatted beside the bearded man, felt for a pulse in his neck, and listened to his chest before straightening up. 'What's your name, soldier?' he asked quietly.

'Wilkins, sir. Private Wilkins.'

The Doctor nodded, his face grim. 'Well, Wilkins, how does it feel to have killed someone?'

Wilkins looked down at the dead man. All the colour had drained from his face. 'Not good, sir,' he said in a small voice. 'Pretty terrible, in fact.'

'Glad to hear it,' said the Doctor. He walked over to Wilkins and patted him on the shoulder.

Wilkins seemed unable to stop looking down at the man he had killed. In a small voice, he asked, 'What was wrong with him?'

'His cells are mutating,' the Doctor said, then corrected himself. '*Were* mutating.'

'Is it a disease?'

'No, there's a sort of... invisible poison in the air.'

Wilkins looked around fearfully, as if he might catch a glimpse of it, swirling like fog. 'Is that going to happen to all of us?' he asked.

'Not if I can help it,' said the Doctor. 'At the moment the leakage is minimal. Those affected must either have been close to the source or are particularly susceptible to zytron waves.'

'I think this is what's happening to Major Daker,' said Wilkins bleakly.

'Major Daker?' Donna had mentioned a Major Daker when she'd been filling him in on what had happened to her yesterday.

'He's my commanding officer. He's not himself. And he's got these lumps on his head.'

'He needs to be isolated and restrained,' the Doctor said. 'Zytron waves affect the mind, turn people violent.' Suddenly he was up on his toes, eager to be off. 'I'll leave you to sort that, shall I?'

'Where are *you* going?' Wilkins asked, out of his depth.

'Packed day ahead. Aliens to track down, disasters to avert. Busy, busy, busy. See ya.'

And with that he was gone.

Donna was taking Tiffin in the garden with Mary, Adelaide and Cameron. It was all very genteel: wicker chairs, a white linen tablecloth, a proper china tea service like her gran used to have. There was even a lace doily over the sugar bowl to keep the flies off, and a three-tiered silver thingy with cakes on it like you got in posh tea shops.

Adelaide and her mother were sipping tea out of dainty cups, but Donna and Cameron had gone for the home-made lemonade, a big jug of which was sitting in the centre of the table, filled with rapidly melting ice cubes and chunks of real lemon. If it hadn't been for the exotic blooms in the flowerbeds edging the immaculately clipped lawn, Donna could almost have believed she was sitting in an English country garden on a baking summer's day. Before coming out, she had asked Adelaide if she'd got any factor 40, but Adelaide hadn't known what she was talking about. Donna had therefore been careful to position herself in the expansive shadow of the large, tasselled parasol above their table.

For the last few minutes, Adelaide had been telling Donna about her work at the camp. Suddenly she yawned. 'Now that the excitement has died down, I really ought to get some sleep,' she said, 'otherwise I shall be all fingers and thumbs tonight.'

Mary Campbell pursed her lips. 'I wish you wouldn't go to that awful place,' she said. 'You'll end up with some ghastly disease.'

Donna could tell from the look on Adelaide's face that this was an old argument.

'The people there need our help, Mother,' she said. 'We can't simply abandon them.'

Mary Campbell sniffed. 'I don't see why not. They managed perfectly well before we arrived. I mean, it's not even as if they're *grateful*.'

Donna felt her hackles rising. 'How do you know?' she said.

Mary blinked at her. 'I beg your pardon?'

'How do you know they're not grateful when you've never even been there?'

Mary reddened. Both Adelaide and Cameron looked at their mother to see how she would respond. When she placed her teacup back in its saucer, it clinked and rattled.

'I've lived in India for twenty years,' she said haughtily. 'I know perfectly well what the people are like. And I know that when you try to offer them help, they simply throw it back in your face.'

'And you offer them help… how?' asked Donna.

'By attempting to instil them with the correct values, of course. By bringing civilisation and stability to the country.'

Donna shook her head 'Yeah, well, maybe they don't want your *values*. Maybe they've got their own values and their own way of doing things.'

Mary's face was flushed. Her hands were trembling as they gripped the arms of her chair. 'I refuse to be harangued like this in my own home!' she exclaimed.

Adelaide said softly, 'Mother *has* had rather a trying morning, Donna. Perhaps it might be best to drop the subject.'

Donna was silent a moment longer, then she said,

'Yeah, sorry.'

Mary gave a stiff nod, and for a moment no one said anything. The awkward atmosphere was broken by an excitable voice from the direction of the house.

'Miss Adelaide! Miss Donna!'

They turned to see Ranjit running across the lawn towards them, waving something in the air. Behind Ranjit, on the porch, Gopal appeared to be attempting to placate a clearly agitated Becharji. He raised his hands, as if to indicate that he would deal with the situation, and then he hurried across the lawn in Ranjit's wake.

Donna grinned at the little Indian boy, taking a secret delight in Mary Campbell's outraged expression as he ran barefoot towards them. 'Hello, Ranjit,' she said, and then she noticed what he was holding in his hand. 'Blimey, where did you get that from?'

Ranjit thumped to a stop and stood there, panting. All at once he seemed to realise that he had broken any number of unwritten social rules by bursting in on them like this. He looked at Mary Campbell's imperious expression and hunched his shoulders, as if he expected to be punished for his insolence.

'It… it is Mr Doctor's,' he mumbled, fixing his gaze on the sonic screwdriver in his hand.

'Yeah, I know that,' said Donna. 'I just wondered what you were doing with it?'

'I didn't steal it, Miss Donna,' Ranjit said in alarm.

'Never thought you did, sweetheart,' she said soothingly. 'Look, why don't you sit down and have some lemonade?'

Ranjit looked at her in astonishment.

'Come on,' she said, reaching for the jug. 'Tell us all about it. Hutch up, Cameron. There's room for both of you on there.'

With a dazed look on his face, Ranjit came forward to share Cameron's chair. Cameron grinned at his friend, and Adelaide too looked amused by Ranjit's reaction. Only Mary Campbell's expression remained frosty.

'Begging your pardon, ladies,' said Gopal, who had now reached the table and was wringing his hands in embarrassment. 'I am so terribly sorry to burst in on you like this.'

'No problem, Gopal,' Donna said, as if it was her house. 'Come and have a cup of tea and a bit of cake.'

She poured him a cup of tea. He looked bemused, but accepted it gratefully.

'Right then, Ranjit,' she said, nodding at the sonic, 'tell me what you're doing with that.'

In the study, the discussion between Gandhi and Sir Edgar was nearing its end. In truth, very little had been achieved. Sir Edgar was standing in front of the fireplace, his meaty hands clasped behind his back. Gandhi was perched on a fat leather armchair, looking out of place among the plush furnishings and the wall-mounted glass cases filled with stuffed birds.

'I sympathise with your position, of course, Mr Gandhi,' Sir Edgar said blithely, 'but I'm afraid there is very little that I can do. Frankly, within a month my colleagues and I will be leaving India for good. How you and your fellow countrymen run things after we've gone is your own concern.'

Gandhi remained as serene as ever. He nodded sagely and said, 'In that case, Mr Campbell, I see only one course of action open to me. I must undertake another fast, a fast unto death, in the hope that it will bring my countrymen to their senses.'

Sir Edgar raised his bristling eyebrows. 'Is that a threat, Mr Gandhi?'

'Only to myself,' Gandhi said with a smile.

Sir Edgar scowled, as though the little man was employing some underhand tactic that he couldn't quite work out. 'But look here, Mr Gandhi, what on Earth do you hope to achieve by starving yourself?'

Gandhi was silent for a moment, as though wondering how best to explain his actions. Finally he said, 'What you must understand, Mr Campbell, is that my relationship with the people of my country is not a political one, but spiritual and emotional. Although I consider myself unworthy of the honour, I know that to them I am "Mahatma" – the Great Soul. When I fast, therefore, politics becomes unimportant and disputes become trivial. The only thing that matters to the people is that my life is saved.' He said all this with no trace of smugness or self-satisfaction.

Sir Edgar said, 'That's quite a power you wield there.'

Gandhi shrugged. 'I don't see it as power. I see it merely as my most effective means of persuasion. And if it fails, at least I am the only one who truly suffers by it.'

Their conversation was interrupted by what sounded like a scuffle in the corridor outside. Sir Edgar heard a voice he didn't recognise say, 'Don't you worry about it. You just go and polish the family silver or something.'

The door opened and a man entered, a skinny man in a tight-fitting blue suit. He looked around and said, '*Nice* place you've got here. Yeah, lovely. Little colonial bolt-hole, away from the hoi polloi. And I see you're a birdwatcher – or maybe you just like killing 'em? Don't agree with it myself, big blokes armed to the teeth, taking it out on small, defenceless creatures which have just as much right to breathe the planet's air as they do. But hey ho, each to his own. Anyway, I'm the Doctor, and you must be Sir Edgar. Hello, Mohandas. Always a pleasure to see *you*. Hope you've recovered from this morning's little escapade.'

All of this was delivered at a rattling pace, the Doctor interspersing his chatter with grins, winks and waves

from the comfort of a fire-warmed room into the icy bleakness of a winter's night. 'How dare you, sir,' he said again. 'How dare you enter my home and speak to me in this manner. Who the blazes are you, anyway? You're nothing but a… a madman come in off the streets, full of wild stories and ridiculous ideas.'

The Doctor stared long and hard at Sir Edgar, and then he said dismissively, 'Oh, you're just an idiot.' He turned his attention to Gandhi, who was still sitting quietly in the plump, shiny armchair.

'Mohandas,' he said, 'will *you* help me?'

Gandhi was already nodding, as though for him the Doctor's credentials and the truth of his words had never been in doubt.

'Of course, Doctor,' he said. 'I will call a meeting to address the people, and I will ask them to listen to you.'

'Thank you,' the Doctor said, pressing his palms together.

Sir Edgar snorted. 'Mr Gandhi, surely you're not going to take this nonsense seriously? The man's clearly a charlatan.'

The Doctor shot him a glance that was both casual and annoyed. 'Oh, put a sock in it, Eddie. You're not worth talking to.' Without even bothering to wait for Sir Edgar's apoplectic response, he stepped past Becharji and across the room to the French windows. Throwing them open he yelled, 'Oi, Donna!' and waved as she turned her head.

'Doctor!' she exclaimed gleefully, rising to her feet.

'Two sugars,' he shouted. Next moment he was strolling across the lawn, hands in pockets. A small figure raced across the grass to meet him.

'Mr Doctor! Mr Doctor!'

'Hiya, Ranjit,' the Doctor said. 'What you got there?' Then a big grin spread across his face. 'Awww, I've been looking for you, you little minx,' he said, taking the sonic from Ranjit and waggling it in front of his nose. 'Where did you get to then?'

'I found it, Mr Doctor. You dropped it on the ground and a boy took it, but I chased him and got it back for you.'

Breathlessly Ranjit told his story. The Doctor was almost at the table when he stopped dead.

'Say that bit again.'

'What bit?'

'The bit about the men coming. The half-made men.'

Patiently Ranjit repeated his story.

'I bet he's got a trace on it,' the Doctor said.

'Who?' asked Donna.

'Whoever's using Calcutta as a zytron fuel dump.' He tapped the sonic against his chin. 'He's probably tuned in to the activation signal … so if I just turn it on… risky I suppose, but… it'd be route one… save a lot of mucking about…' He frowned, then nodded decisively. 'Yeah, why not? He who dares and all that.'

'What *are* you prattling on about?' Donna asked.

Instead of replying, the Doctor turned and ran back to the centre of the lawn.

'What are you doing *now*?' Donna shouted in frustration.

'Just wanna try something. Stand well back, and keep the pot warm.'

'What do you mean? Where are you going?'

'Let's see, shall we?'

The Doctor held the sonic above his head and turned it on. Almost immediately there was a silvery shimmer in the air, and suddenly he was surrounded by a quartet of chalk-white men with blank features and no eyes.

Mary Campbell's hand flew to her mouth; Adelaide screamed; Gopal and the boys goggled in terror. Donna yelled, 'Doctor!' and half-rose from her seat.

The Doctor stood there calmly, looking around at the creatures as they closed in on him.

'Take me to your leader,' he said as the men grabbed him.

There was another shimmer, and a second later the Doctor and the four men had disappeared.

NINE

The journey was almost instantaneous. One second the Doctor was standing on a springy green lawn, bathed in bright sunshine, the next he was in chilly darkness with a stony surface beneath his feet.

Two of the creatures that had transported him here held his arms in a light grip. What this told him was that they – or rather, whoever was controlling them – knew that even if he tried to give them the slip he wouldn't get far. Although the creatures were holding him, they didn't prevent him from switching off his sonic and slipping it back into his pocket. With the lightest of nudges, they ushered him along what he could only assume was a subterranean passage.

He was angry. And the reason he was angry was because the instant the creatures had appeared in the garden he had recognised them. Or rather, he had recognised the cruel and illegal process by which they had been created.

Throughout the universe the creatures were known by many different names, but most commonly as gelem warriors. They were a construct race, and their shape depended on whichever species had been harvested to provide the raw material. Their creation, the Doctor knew, had been outlawed by the Pact of Chib in the equivalent of Earth's eleventh century. Many of the emergent space-faring races had used gelem warriors as cannon fodder in the initial skirmishes of what had later become known as the War of the Five Hundred Worlds. These races would harvest the planets of more primitive species and subject their populations to a hideously painful process, in which their basest instincts were siphoned off in extraction machines and used to create a new race of remorseless, merciless troops. Gelem warriors could survive extreme heat and cold, and needed neither to breathe, eat, drink nor sleep. In essence they were machine-creatures made of pseudo-flesh and powered by a single-minded core of obedience, hatred and aggression. They were like Daleks without the intelligence, efficient but expendable. Perhaps the most horrifying aspect of all was that it took at least five members of a species to create each gelem warrior. Five living creatures had to die horribly to produce one unthinking monster.

The Doctor's footsteps echoed hollowly as he was marched through a maze of passageways. His guess was that he was in a pretty sizeable cave system, not far from Calcutta. The caves were narrow and pitch black, though there was a strong flow-through of air, suggesting there had to be plenty of openings up on the surface. A human being wouldn't have been able to see anything in the darkness, but the Doctor's superior eyesight was able to discern the basic layout of the route ahead as a series of shadowy shapes.

Eventually the Doctor and his captors came to a halt in front of what appeared to be a section of solid wall. One of the gelem warriors stretched out a hand and touched the wall, and instantly it shimmered and disappeared. The group passed through into a small chamber, which looked like the glowing guts of some vast machine. The chamber was oddly shaped, its gleaming black walls composed of strange, jagged angles. The Doctor whipped out his black-framed spectacles and peered curiously at the exposed tangle of machinery around him.

The technology was advanced, but the craft itself was old, and appeared to have been patched and re-patched over many years. What was even more interesting was that the confused mass of interlinked metal and plastic was not the product of a single planet. There was evidence, even in this tiny area, to suggest that defective systems had been kept operational by fusing them with ostensibly non-compatible components. The Doctor examined a delicate array of filaments that appeared to have been welded to a spiky metal starfish, and shook his head like an electrician faced with a bit of dodgy DIY.

'Surely that's not… Oh, blimey, it is. An artificial synapse modulator's impulse strands are being sieved through the clamp mechanism of a Cassian neutron scoop. That's brilliant! But totally bonkers! Doesn't whoever's done this realise the neural feedback could cause lockdown in the… Oh, hang on, he's draining off the excess with a suction filter from a Draconian land cruiser. Well… all right, that *is* impressive, I'll give him that. But this old crate would still never pass its MOT.'

A door opened on the far side of the chamber, five triangular spars of shiny black material folding back like the petals of a flower to create a space through which they could pass. The Doctor was ushered along a cramped series of weirdly proportioned corridors, all the while shaking his head and tut-tutting at the way in which different alien technologies had been cannibalised to keep the craft airworthy. At any one time he was able to spot about a thousand things that were teetering on the brink of going wrong, all of which added up to a countless number of potential disasters just waiting to happen.

At last he was pushed into a space about the size of

an average sitting room. Pulsing strands and filaments attached to random bits of equipment snaked and looped everywhere, though they all seemed to lead to the same place – a complicated, web-like framework in the centre of the room, which contained the ship's pilot.

'So you're the nutjob behind this lot,' said the Doctor, glaring up at the alien quivering like a spider at the centre of its web of technology. 'I'm disappointed. I thought the Jal Karath were supposed to be peace-loving and intelligent.'

The creature was black, sinuous and weed-like. It was composed of dozens of thin, twining limbs, attached to a thicker central stalk, which was covered in clusters of blinking, milky-white eyes. Via its limbs, it was linked into the workings of the spacecraft, giving the impression that the vessel was an extension of its body, or even that the creature itself formed the engine, or perhaps the heart, of its ship.

'So we are,' the alien said, its voice high and fluting, but oddly machine-like, as though it was being relayed through some mechanical device.

'Well, you coulda fooled me,' said the Doctor. 'With your gelem warriors and your zytron dumping, you're like a one-organism bio-hazard.'

'I am not responsible for either of these… misdemeanours,' said the Jal Karath blithely.

The Doctor pointed an accusatory finger at the alien.

'There's no point trying to wriggle out of it, sunshine. I've got you bang to rights. And I'll tell you what. I'm gonna put an end to this, right here, right now. And no amount of your ghoulish, gormless gelem warriors will be able to stop me.'

The Jal Karath seemed unconcerned by the Doctor's threat. 'Your bio-scan reveals that you are not a native of this planet.'

'So?' said the Doctor. 'What's that got to do with the price of walnuts?'

'I'm curious. What does the fate of these primitives matter to you?'

'They're living, feeling, intelligent creatures,' said the Doctor angrily, 'and living, feeling, intelligent creatures have the right not to be terrorised and murdered by other living, feeling, intelligent creatures. Just cos they're not as brainy as you doesn't mean—'

'I agree,' said the Jal Karath.

The Doctor stopped, cut off in mid-sentence. 'What?'

'I agree that these primitive creatures have the right to live their lives in peace, free from interference by other species. That is why I am here.'

'Right,' said the Doctor heavily. 'Well, see, the thing is, I think you're missing the point. It's *because* you're here that all this bad stuff is happening.'

'No it isn't,' said the Jal Karath.

The Doctor shook his head. 'Crikey, you've got

some serious denial issues. Look, shall we rewind this conversation? Start at the beginning? I'll try and air my grievances in words of one syllable, so you can understand.'

'I understand perfectly well,' said the Jal Karath in its fluting and infuriatingly reasonable voice. 'It is you who does not understand; you who is making assumptions about my presence on this planet.'

The Doctor sighed, raised one eyebrow and folded his arms. 'All right, I'll buy that for now. Go on. Surprise me.'

The Jal Karath stirred in its pulsing web. Its multiple eyes blinked. 'My name is Darac-Poul-Caparrel-Jal-7. I am a Hive 7 Enforcer. I am here in pursuit of a fugitive from my planet, Veec-Elic-Savareen-Jal-9. Veec-9 is wanted for terrorist crimes against all eleven Hives on Jal Paloor. He is using stolen glamour technology to live among the primitives on this planet. His intention is to harvest enough of these primitives—'

'Humans,' said the Doctor bluntly. 'They're called humans.'

'Enough of these *humans*,' continued the Jal Karath, 'to build an army of gelem warriors. He intends to use his army to overthrow the eleven Hives and establish a dictatorship. It is my mission to stop him.'

'What, just you?' said the Doctor. 'In a battered old crate like this? The eleven Hives a bit strapped for cash, are they?'

The Jal Karath did not react to the Doctor's mocking tone. Its trilling voice, which reminded the Doctor of the squeak of fingernails on an icy window, remained calm and constant.

'There were four of us when we set out on this mission, each one carefully selected by the Hive Council. This "battered old crate", as you call it, was once an A-class pulse flier, the most technologically advanced isomorphic craft ever produced on Jal Paloor.'

The Doctor whistled. 'You must have been up in the air for a very long time.'

'When I left Jal Paloor my civilisation was in the ninety-third quadrant.'

'So that's…' the Doctor did a quick calculation '… over four hundred years ago. What happened to your mates?'

'They expired when their craft's systems failed. They are in the Drift now.'

'And meanwhile you keep limping along,' said the Doctor. 'Why don't you just do yourself a favour, Darac-7? Why don't you give it all up and go home?'

'We are a long-lived race,' said the Jal Karath, 'and on Jal Paloor little changes from one quadrant to the next. As long as Veec-9 is alive, he is a danger to us.'

The Doctor regarded the alien pilot, stony-faced. 'That doesn't excuse your use of gelem warriors to track down this fugitive of yours. Extraction machines were outlawed centuries ago. According to article 29.8 of the Shadow Proclamation—'

'The gelem warriors are not mine,' said the Jal Karath.

'Blimey, you lot are rude!' the Doctor exclaimed indignantly. 'Always butting in.' He nodded at the silent white figures behind him. 'So what are this lot then? Scotch mist?'

'These creatures were created by Veec-9. I was able to intercept and reprogram them as search units.'

'And when you detected my sonic you thought it was Veec-9 using stolen technology, so you sent them to pick him up?'

'Quite so.'

'But instead you got me. Just an innocent bloke passing through.'

The Jal Karath was silent for a moment. Then it said, 'Your bio scan confirms that you are not a native of this world, but my scanner is unable to identify your planet of origin.'

'Well, I'm not surprised,' said the Doctor glibly. 'I mean, look at this mess. I bet half your systems are on the blink.' He leaned forward to examine a dial linked to one of the pulsing strands of web and gave it a tap. 'How are your zytron shields?' he asked casually.

'My zytron shields?'

'Yeah. Cos the thing is, zytron energy is leaking out of somewhere like nobody's business. People are dropping like flies. And if that's down to you, then galactic law states that your vehicle could be impounded. If you're found negligent, you might even get banged up on one of the prison planets. As I'm sure you know, Darac-7, zytron energy is *very* nasty stuff. And the authorities come down like a ton of bricks on pilots who—'

'My shielding is fine,' said the Jal Karath quickly. 'The safety of the indigenous population of any planet on which I make landfall is of paramount importance to me. If *my* craft was leaking harmful elements into the atmosphere my pulse sensors would inform me of it immediately.'

'Not if your pulse sensors were playing up, they wouldn't.'

'I assure you...what *is* your name?'

'Just call me Doctor.'

'I assure you, Doctor, that the problem does not lie with my vessel. Veec-9's vessel is old, decrepit—'

'What, even compared to this one?' said the Doctor rudely.

The Jal Karath fell silent. The Doctor looked up at it, eyes narrowed. At last he said, 'All right, let's say I accept what you're telling me. How will Veec-9 create and transport a whole army of gelem warriors? I mean, that's a heck of an undertaking for a single bloke in a one-man ship.'

'The latest intelligence transmitted from the eleven

Hives informs me that Veec-9 will not create the majority of his warriors on this world,' replied the Jal Karath. 'He will use the small number of warriors he has created here to harvest his required number of the planet's population. Until he is ready to depart he will imprison these captives within a stasis barrier contained behind a glamour shield. When the time comes he will use funds supplied by his misguided supporters to employ mercenaries, who will transport the prisoners to the planet – one of the many thousands of dead planets which surround Jal Paloor – where he has established his base. That is where the extraction process will take place. Although we know this, what we do not know is on precisely which planet Veec-9 is building up his forces. Any one of them would be ideally positioned for launching an attack on the home world.'

Grimly the Doctor asked, 'And what is his "required number" of humans?'

'We believe that Veec-9 hopes to yield at least ten thousand gelem warriors from each planet he harvests.'

'Fifty thousand people,' said the Doctor quietly, his voice burning with fury. 'Fifty thousand lives snuffed out in those filthy machines. And this is just the place to suck up the raw material, isn't it? The poor of India – the sick, the downtrodden, the dispossessed. No one will miss them. They're already non-people, forgotten and unmourned. Fifty thousand terrified human beings ending their lives millions of miles from home: snatched up, packed into storage crates, chewed and spat out, like so much gristle.' The Doctor's eyes were black, as black as endless night, and yet at the same time somehow blazing with fire. 'Well, that's not gonna happen. Not on my watch.'

He drew in a long breath, as though storing his rage deep inside. Turning to the Jal Karath, he said, 'Why haven't you traced the zytron leakage from Veec-9's ship back to its source?'

The alien shivered in its web, perhaps in response to the Doctor's cold fury, perhaps because it was merely receiving data through its interlinked systems. It said, 'The glamour is concealing it. I can pick up hot-spots of zytron energy, but not the ship itself.'

'Hmm,' said the Doctor. 'And just as a matter of interest, was that your ship in the temple today?'

The Jal Karath blinked its many eyes. 'No, Doctor. The craft must have belonged to Veec-9. I have remained in this location since I made landfall.'

'I see. And where *are* we, exactly?'

'I don't know. Somewhere beneath the ground. Somewhere safe.'

'But if Veec-9 is wandering around disguised as a human and you're skulking down here, how are you gonna find him?'

'My reprogrammed warriors are primed, Doctor. I

have initiated a technology scan. When Veec-9 reveals his position, my warriors will be ready.'

'But what if he *doesn't* reveal his position?' the Doctor said. 'What if he keeps all his technology tucked away behind that glamour of his – which you can't penetrate?'

'Then the chase will go on, Doctor. Into the stars.'

The Doctor rubbed his chin absently. 'Yeah, you see, that's all very well, Darac-7, but, according to you, Veec-9 won't head off into the wild blue yonder until he's got fifty thousand humans tucked safely under his belt. And personally I'm not prepared to wait that long. So why don't you leave this one up to me, eh? I'll sort it.'

'What will you do, Doctor?' the alien asked warily.

'Well, I don't wanna boast, but my scanners are a lot bigger than your scanners. And now that I've got my sonic back, I can pinpoint the source of the zytron leakage by inputting the readings from my ship.'

Again the Jal Karath was silent, as though considering the Doctor's proposal.

Finally it said, 'Veec-9 is a dangerous adversary, Doctor. If he finds out you are helping me, he will try to kill you.'

'Yeah, well, I'm used to that,' said the Doctor airily. 'People try to kill me all the time.'

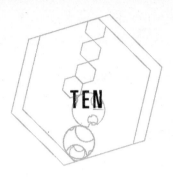

TEN

Back at the Campbells' house, the Doctor's disappearance had created uproar. Mary Campbell had fainted, or at least swooned, and had had to be carried indoors by Becharji and several servants; Gopal, clearly uncomfortable and out of place, had made his excuses and left at the earliest opportunity, taking Ranjit with him; Cameron had been sent indoors 'for his own safety', even though there was no evidence that indoors was any safer than outdoors; and now only Donna and Adelaide were left in the garden, Donna clinging to the hope that the Doctor would reappear in the same place he had vanished, and Adelaide – despite all the excitement – snoozing in her chair in the sun, having finally succumbed to fatigue after working a full overnight shift at the camp.

Donna didn't really know what to do. She felt a bit of a spare part just sitting and waiting, and was all too aware that she couldn't mooch around here for ever. She was annoyed with the Doctor for going off without her yet again. Even if he was in danger, she would rather be with him than hanging about not knowing what was going on.

Several times since she'd started travelling with the Doctor, it had occurred to her to wonder what she'd do if anything happened to him. She would just have to get on with things, she supposed. But it frightened her that she had no identity in this period – no family, no friends, no roots. Most of the time, life with the Doctor was a rollercoaster ride, but occasionally it struck her how lost and alone she would be without him. He was her ticket home – her *only* ticket home. And, however fantastic it was to roam time and space in his company, she still needed the reassurance that home would be there waiting for her whenever she decided she wanted to pop back for a visit.

Her reverie was interrupted by movement in her peripheral vision. She turned to see Gandhi approaching from the direction of the house, walking across the grass towards her.

She smiled. His was a serene presence, which immediately made her feel better.

'Hiya,' she said when he was close enough.

He smiled and pressed his palms together. 'Do you

mind if I join you?'

'I'd love you to. Pull up a pew.'

He did so, sitting down with a creak of wicker.

'Lemonade?' Donna asked.

'Thank you, no.'

She nodded vaguely towards the middle of the lawn. 'Did you see what happened?'

'I only heard about it. Everyone is very excitable. It sounds as though it was a most extraordinary occurrence.'

Donna shrugged. 'I s'pose so. Stuff like that happens to the Doctor all the time. It just gets annoying after a while.'

There was a moment of silence, then Gandhi said, 'You are worried about him.' It was a statement rather than a question.

Donna shrugged. 'I'm sure he'll be fine. He's been in a lot worse scrapes than this. But… yeah. Yeah I am.'

'The Doctor is a seeker of truth,' said Gandhi. 'And God is truth. Therefore he is in good company.'

Donna looked at his gentle face, his eyes big, almost childlike, behind his spectacles, and she broke into a smile. 'I don't know what you're on about half the time,' she said, 'but the way you say things, it just makes me feel better. You and the Doctor, you're alike in a lot of ways.'

Gandhi chuckled. 'I will take that as the greatest of compliments.'

Suddenly the large white house at the edge of the lawn seemed to blur, as though in a heat haze. Donna turned her head, and saw a silvery shimmer in the centre of the lawn, like a scene viewed through a smeared window. She rose from her seat as the Doctor reappeared, accompanied by two of the chalk-white figures.

'Cheers, fellers,' he said distractedly, and then he began striding across the lawn towards the house, his face grim.

'Oi, hang on!' Donna shouted, running after him. She half-turned to Gandhi. 'Sorry about this, Mohandas.'

He raised a hand, indicating that she had no need to apologise, and that she should go after the Doctor. She turned again just in time to see the chalk-men shimmer and disappear. 'Wait up, you!' she yelled. 'Don't you dare leave me behind again.'

He stopped abruptly, allowing her to catch up. He glanced at her, frowning.

'You've got that face on,' she said.

'What face?'

'Like you're gonna slap someone.'

He was silent for a moment, then he said, 'Yeah, well, maybe I am.' He began walking again.

'I've been worried sick about you. At least tell me where you've been?'

He scowled at her, and then he sighed, his expression softening. 'How worried were you? On a scale of one to ten? One being couldn't care less, and ten being completely inconsolable?'

She shrugged. 'Dunno. Four maybe.'

'*Four!*' he exclaimed, his voice high-pitched with indignation. 'That's charming, that is. You do your best to save someone's planet and they're not even bothered.'

She slapped his arm. 'Oh, all right. Five then.' Abruptly she gave him a fierce hug. 'You do my head in, you do.'

He hugged her back, then extracted himself with a grin. 'Come on,' he said, 'let's walk. I'll tell you about it as we go.'

'Where we going?' she asked.

'TARDIS,' he replied.

'Oh. We off then?'

'You might be,' he replied cheekily, 'but I'm as fresh as a daisy.'

Adelaide decided that she would just have to lump it. Best-laid plans, and all that. When she had arrived home that morning she had wanted nothing more than a quick bite to eat and a nice long nap, but the day had not worked out quite as she had envisaged.

In the end she had managed to grab no more than a snooze in a garden chair, and even then she had no idea how she had managed to nod off, what with the drama of the Doctor turning up and then being whisked away by those ghastly creatures. Some time later she had woken with a start, stiff-necked and achy-backed, to find that her previous companion, Donna, had now been replaced by Mr Gandhi, who had been sitting cross-legged on the ground in a state of apparent meditation.

As soon as she had jerked awake he had opened one eye, smiled and said hello. It turned out his meeting with her father was over, and he had been waiting patiently for her to wake up in order to invite her to share a tonga with him back to the camp. Adelaide had hurriedly washed and changed, and twenty minutes later the two of them were sitting side by side, she feeling a little woozy and wondering how she was going to get through another gruelling night shift.

By the time they arrived back, Mr Gandhi had filled her in on what she had missed during her doze. He told her about the Doctor's reappearance and about his and Donna's abrupt departure.

Now Adelaide was back at work, tending to the sick and wounded and trying not to think about how tired she was. She was in one of the medical tents, helping Edward dress a particularly nasty head wound, when they heard shouts and screams from outside.

They looked at each other in alarm.

'What on Earth…?' Edward said.

The camp had been established as a sanctuary, a place which catered for all religions and castes, but

Edward and Adelaide were not naive enough to think that this meant they were exempt from attack. They knew there were still plenty of fanatics who believed that each strata of Indian society should remain within its own separate enclave, and who were prepared to go to extreme lengths to make their point. Even Gandhi had come in for criticism by those of his own people who were appalled not only by the fact that he mixed with 'untouchables', but that he had even described them as Harijans – Children of God.

'You stay here, my dear,' Edward said, and hurried to the tent entrance.

'My eye,' Adelaide muttered, though she left it a few seconds before going after him.

It was early evening, but not yet dark, or anywhere near. As Adelaide stepped outside, a harsh white disc of sun still shone down from a cloudless sky, illuminating the terrible scene before her.

Like blemishes on her vision, the air was full of silvery shimmers, and chalk-white men, identical to the ones which had materialised on her lawn that afternoon, were appearing all over the camp. Naturally, their presence was causing widespread panic. People were shouting and screaming, fleeing in all directions, trampling over one another's shelters and even each other to get away.

It was immediately evident why the hideous figures were there. Adelaide saw them grabbing people at random – men, women and children – and simply vanishing with them, just as they had with the Doctor. They seemed to hunt in pairs, and their numbers remained constant; as one pair disappeared with a victim, or sometimes two victims, another pair would shimmer into existence. Although people were running hither and thither, for the chalk-men the operation was clearly akin to shooting fish in a barrel. Sometimes the air would shimmer and they would appear directly in the path of someone who would then be unable to prevent him- or herself running straight into their clutches. To Adelaide it looked like a battlefield, albeit a bloodless one, or one of those dreadful depictions of Hell by the artist Hieronymus Bosch.

She saw Edward in the crowd, running towards a pair of chalk-men who were bearing down on a small girl of around six years old. The girl was standing transfixed, like a bird mesmerised by a snake. Edward was clutching his old service revolver, its muzzle pointing at the sky.

He shouted something, but in the general cacophony of panic-stricken voices Adelaide couldn't make out his words. It was clearly a challenge, however, for a moment later he lowered his gun and fired at one of the chalk-men. The shot made a loud crack in the early evening air. To her horror, Adelaide saw the chalk-man stagger as a black bullet hole appeared on the left side of his chest, just beneath his collar bone. More horrifying still was the fact that the shot barely slowed the creature down. Almost immediately he straightened up and resumed his remorseless advance.

Edward loosed off another two shots, hitting the same man in the chest once again, and then his partner in the stomach. When this too had minimal effect, he raised his gun butt-first and ran at the men, as though fully intending to club them unconscious with it.

He was too late to save the girl. Even as he ran forward, one of the chalk-men reached out and grabbed her arm. An instant later the chalk-man and the girl shimmered and vanished.

'You filthy…' Edward yelled, his voice carrying above the screams and shouts of the crowd. He reached the second chalk-man and brought his revolver down in a savage arc towards the creature's hairless skull.

Adelaide winced, anticipating the impact, but with blinding speed the chalk-man's hand shot up and grabbed Edward's arm before the gun could connect. A look of horror, rage and disbelief appeared on Edward's face – and then he and the chalk-man also vanished.

Adelaide's hand flew to her mouth. Desperately she wondered what to do. It was pointless trying to flee through the camp, just as it was pointless joining the mêlée with the intention of giving aid. In the end she decided to go back into the tent and take shelter. Once the mayhem was over, she would seek out the Doctor and Donna and tell them what had happened.

There was something about the Doctor. Something authoritative and reassuring. She felt instinctively that he would know what to do. Turning, she lifted aside the flap of canvas and re-entered the tent.

She barely had time to register the eyeless face of the chalk-man looming over her before the creature reached out and grabbed her arm.

Adelaide struggled, but it was no use. The chalk-man's grip was like iron. She felt a weird kind of wrenching sensation and then the world dissolved around her.

'So do you believe this Jal Karath thing then?'

Donna was hot, sweaty and irritable. The Doctor had kept up a pretty mean pace on the long walk back to the TARDIS, and she had been determined not to be a hindrance by slowing him down. He had that look on his face that he got when she knew someone was in for it. This was when he was at his rudest, when he was least tolerant of people being stupid or obstructive or not pulling their weight.

'I'm operating on the assumption that he was telling the truth,' he said, and added after a pause. 'But that he might not have been.'

'Thanks,' she said heavily, 'that makes everything *much* clearer.' She made an exasperated sound and flapped her hands in front of her face.

The Doctor glanced at her. 'Seen someone you

know?'

'It's these flies,' she said.

'Can't say I've ever been friends with a fly.' He looked thoughtful. 'Knew some butterflies once. And beetles. I've chatted to loads of beetles. Never a good idea to accept a dinner invitation from one, though.'

'I'll bear that in mind,' said Donna.

They rounded a corner and the Doctor grinned suddenly. 'Have I got a brilliant sense of direction or what?'

There was the TARDIS, standing where they had left it in the shadows at the end of a quiet, narrow alley.

'Home from home,' she said. 'So what happens next? We get the readings from the TARDIS…'

'Focus in on them with the sonic, and… *spa-twang!*'

'Spa-twang?' she repeated.

'Technical term. Think of the zytron trail like a long elastic band at full stretch. And think of the TARDIS like a stone in the loop of the band. Soon as the sonic converts the readings into coordinates and feeds them back into the TARDIS, off we go… *spa-twang!*'

'Sounds painful.'

'Nah, it'll be fun. Long as we're strapped in tight there's nothing that can go wrong. Well… almost nothing.'

Now that the TARDIS was in sight, he stretched his legs, putting on an extra spurt of speed. Donna struggled to keep up, still swiping irritably at the flies buzzing around her head. He was fumbling in his pocket for the key when suddenly there was a silvery shimmer in the air.

Next moment, four gelem warriors were standing in front of the TARDIS, facing them.

The Doctor stopped, looking warily at the white figures. Almost absently he reached out a long arm and shielded Donna with it, positioning his body in front of hers.

'Do you think they'll attack?' she hissed.

'Dunno,' he murmured. 'Doubt they're here for a chinwag. Gelem warriors are rubbish at conversation, probably cos they never watch telly or read *Heat* magazine – which I know is something *you'll* find hard to believe.'

'Oi,' she said, jabbing him in the back. 'So how do we get past them?'

'We implement my brilliantly conceived plan,' he said.

'Which is?'

'Dunno. Haven't thought of it yet.'

He looked keenly about him, checking out the available resources. However, he had barely begun to do so when the quartet of gelem warriors turned towards the TARDIS and placed their hands on it.

'No!' the Doctor shouted, rushing forward. 'No, no, no, no, no!'

Donna realised what the gelem warriors were doing

a split-second after the Doctor did.

'Oh…' she said, but by the time she had completed the expletive the air had shimmered and the gelem warriors had gone, taking the TARDIS with them.

As two more of the terrible men suddenly appeared, Ranjit turned and dived through the open doorway of a ramshackle lean-to. So far he had escaped capture partly due to good luck and partly because, as everyone else had started to panic, he had managed to keep his head.

Having seen the eyeless men before, he had not been as shocked as everyone else, and so had had the presence of mind to notice two things about them. One was that they didn't run – there were so many people around that they didn't need to – and the other was that they didn't *select* their victims, but simply grabbed whoever was closest.

Ranjit had made it across the camp by keeping low, taking his time and using the shelters for cover. Even so, he had had a couple of near misses when the air had shimmered and the creatures had appeared in front of him. The first time he had escaped by ducking out of sight a split second before the men had fully materialised, and the second time one of them had actually been shooting out a hand in his direction, when a thin, turbaned man had blundered into their path, inadvertently barging into Ranjit and knocking him out of the way.

Now, as Ranjit dived through the doorway of the lean-to, he heard a little scream. He rolled over in the dust and jumped straight to his feet. A girl was huddled in the shadows at the back of the shabby construction, her eyes wide and dark, her knees drawn up to her chin and her clenched fists pressed to her face.

Ranjit raised a finger to his lips and hoped that the girl wasn't too scared to see sense. He hoped too that the eyeless men had not heard her scream. If they came crashing in to investigate the sound there would be no escape for either of them.

He waited for almost a minute, his ears attuned to the slightest movement. However, he could hear nothing above the screams and pounding footsteps of the camp's inhabitants. The eyeless men may have gone or they may simply have been standing outside, waiting patiently for him to emerge. It didn't help that they moved almost silently, like ghosts. He let another thirty seconds slide by, and then he turned to the girl.

'I am going now,' he whispered. 'You stay here. If you wait until all is quiet, I am sure you will be safe.'

The girl stared at him, too scared to nod or even blink.

'Goodbye,' Ranjit said, and then he crept to the entrance of the lean-to and peeked out.

The half-made men were nowhere to be seen. Ranjit breathed a sigh of relief and ran across to the next dilapidated shelter. He kept low and alert as he continued his zigzag progress, and minutes later he reached his destination.

At least two of Gandhi's attendants were usually stationed outside the entrance to his modest shelter on the far edge of the camp, coordinating the large number of people who wished to speak to the Mahatma on a daily basis. Now, though, the shelter was silent and seemingly deserted. Ranjit fervently hoped that Gandhi and his attendants had either fled or that he would find them huddled inside.

His greatest fear was that Bapu had been taken by the eyeless men. Young as he was, Ranjit knew that an India without Gandhi was unthinkable. Peering from right to left, he slipped across to Gandhi's shelter and pressed his face against the ragged sheets of cloth draped across the entrance.

'Bapu,' he hissed urgently. 'Bapu.'

To his surprise, a calm voice said, 'I am here.'

With another quick glance behind him, Ranjit lifted one of the sheets of cloth and slipped inside. Gandhi was sitting cross-legged on the floor, having evidently been in a state of prayer or contemplation.

It was clear that Gandhi was alone, but Ranjit looked around anyway. 'Where are your attendants?'

'They have fled in terror,' Gandhi told him.

'They abandoned you?' Ranjit asked in astonishment.

Gandhi smiled. 'They did not wish to do so, but I insisted that they go. I told them I had no right to be responsible for their fate. I'm afraid, for their own sakes, I was very forceful.' He laughed lightly, as though this was a great joke.

'Why did you not go with them?' Ranjit asked.

'It is not my nature to run away,' Gandhi said. 'I will not fight these foes, but neither will I flee from them. If they find me here, then it is God's will and I will accept it. And if they do not find me here, then that is God's will also.'

Ranjit thought about this for a moment. Then he said, 'I have come to rescue you.'

Gandhi shook his head. 'I do not need to be rescued.'

'What if it is God's will that I rescue you?' Ranjit said.

There was silence for a moment, then Gandhi chuckled. 'How do you *propose* to rescue me?'

'I will lead you away from here along the safest route. I will defend you if necessary.'

'I will not allow anyone to raise their hand in anger in my name,' Gandhi said.

'I will not raise my hand,' Ranjit said. 'I will shield you.' He paused, then added, 'We need you, Bapu. These enemies we face, they are not living enemies. They are *like* men, but they are not men. They are… demons, from another world. They are a threat to us all, and I believe that the only way to defeat them is to stand against them. But to do that we need you and the Doctor to find a way. You are both very wise, and together I know that you can help us. Please, Bapu, come with me.'

Gandhi looked long and hard at the boy, his eyes unblinking behind his spectacles. Finally he raised his hands, palms up, as if placing the matter in the lap of the gods.

'How can I refuse?' he said.

The Doctor was furious. 'Take off your hat,' he snapped at Donna.

'You what?'

'Just do it. Take it off and turn it upside down.'

She glared at him. 'A "please" wouldn't go amiss, y'know.'

He gritted his teeth. '*Please* take off your hat, Donna.'

'Certainly,' she said, removing her wide-brimmed hat and shaking out her long red hair. She held the hat upside down, then her eyes narrowed and she drew it back. 'Hang on, you're not gonna throw up in it, are you?'

He glared at her.

'Sorry,' she said. 'But it wouldn't be the first time that's happened to me.'

He opened his mouth, and then shook his head. 'No,

on second thoughts, I don't think I wanna know.'

He started delving into his jacket pockets, scooping out great handfuls of stuff and dumping them in the hat. Among all the alien bits and pieces were dusty sweets, a bouncy pink ball with Donald Duck's face on it, a rubber spider with three legs missing, an old creased postcard of Brighton Pier, a mass of linked paperclips, weird shells, variously coloured chunks of stone, a cocktail umbrella...

'Is this a general clearout or are you actually looking for something?' she said.

'Tracking device,' he muttered.

'What, to track the TARDIS with?'

'Not *my* tracking device, *their* tracking device.'

She shook her head. 'Sorry, you've lost me.'

He pulled a scratched old cassette box out of his pocket and his face brightened. 'Aw, I wondered where that had gone.'

'What is it?' asked Donna.

'Recording of me and Elvis singing "How Much Is That Doggy In The Window?" We were gonna release it as a single, but Colonel Tom wouldn't let us, grumpy old so and so. Probably just as well, really.' He slipped the cassette into the breast pocket of his jacket and said, 'It wasn't just a coincidence, the gelem warriors appearing like that and nicking the TARDIS. The only way they can have found it was by monitoring my movements. Which means someone, somewhere, must've planted a tracker on me. Unless…'

His head snapped up and he peered intently at Donna.

Discomfited, she said, 'What you staring at me for?'

He didn't reply. Instead he whipped out his sonic, pointed it at her face and turned it on.

Donna flinched, but immediately realised he wasn't actually pointing the sonic *at* her – he was pointing it at something above her head. She looked up, and was just in time to see one of the circling flies shimmer and change into a little whizzing metal object. She jumped back as the thing fizzed and sparked, then dropped out of the air, like a tiny warplane disabled by enemy fire. The Doctor switched off the sonic, stretched out his other hand and caught the thing in his palm. He and Donna leaned forward to have a look at it.

It was a disc of brushed metal about the size of a Smartie. Donna could see a tiny inset propeller and a miniscule lens on the front, like a black dot of an eye.

'Beautiful,' he murmured.

Impressed, Donna said, 'That thing was disguised as a fly?'

The Doctor flipped the disc into the air and caught it again. 'Glamour technology,' he said.

'That's well devious.' She straightened up. 'So what do we do now?'

'Mohandas was gonna call a meeting, address the people. We'll have to use it to spread the word, get everyone looking for the ship.'

'That could take ages.'

A scowl flashed across his face. 'Got any better ideas?'

'No,' she sighed.

'Come on then.' He spun on his heels, and then stopped. 'Oh,' he said.

Donna turned to see what had taken him by surprise, and her eyes widened.

Gopal was standing at the entrance to the alleyway, pointing a gun at them.

ELEVEN

There was a moment of silence, then the Doctor said conversationally, 'That's a Mezon disintegrator 7.5, isn't it?'

Gopal licked his lips. He looked sweaty and nervous. Donna saw that his upraised hand was trembling.

The Doctor shoved his own hands into his pockets and said in the same casual tone, 'You wanna be careful with that. The settings aren't designed for big fat human fingers like yours. Ideally you need to be on 13-85 for close work like this, but I've seen people stick it on 13-89, thinking it won't make a difference. Trouble is, the 89s are the span settings. One false move and Calcutta'll become a big rubble pancake. Course, you're probably not bothered about that, being a ruthless intergalactic warlord and all.'

'I am not a warlord,' muttered Gopal.

'Nah, course you're not,' said the Doctor dismissively. 'I'll bet you're just creating all those gelem warriors to hire out as butlers. Butlers R Us – dinner served, enemies annihilated. You can use that in the brochure if you like. Just give me a credit in the small print.'

Gopal shook his head quickly. 'The gelem warriors are not mine, Doctor. As you well know.'

'Hang on a minute,' Donna butted in before the Doctor could respond. 'Can I just ask before I get totally confused – is Gopal human or alien?'

The Doctor tilted his head back. Despite having a gun pointed at him, he looked not just relaxed but positively cocky. 'He's a Jal Karath,' he said, 'and his name's not Gopal, it's Veec-Elic-Savareen-Jal-9.'

'And he's been using this glamour technology thingy to disguise himself as a human?'

'Yep.'

'So… what does he look like really?'

The Doctor scrunched up his face. 'Well, he's a kind of… black weed. With eyes. Lots of eyes.'

Now it was Donna's turn to pull a face. 'No wonder he's wearing a disguise.' Raising her voice, she shouted, 'Think you're clever, do you, killing all those people? Turning 'em into these gelem things.'

Gopal swung the gun in her direction. The Doctor took a deliberate sideways step into its path, shielding her.

'I have killed nobody,' Gopal protested.

'Course you haven't,' said the Doctor airily. 'Wouldn't harm a fly, you. That's why you're pointing a gun at my noggin.'

'I resort to such measures only because you leave me no choice, Doctor.'

'Really?' the Doctor replied. 'And how do you work that one out?'

Gopal licked his lips. He still looked nervous. Donna saw a line of sweat trickle down his face. 'I know you are in league with Darac-Poul-Caparrel-Jal-7.'

Donna blinked. 'Who's he when he's at home?'

'He's the other Jal Karath I was telling you about,' the Doctor explained.

'The space policeman, you mean?'

Gopal laughed. The sound was hard and bitter. 'Is that what he told you? That he was a Hive 7 Enforcer?'

The Doctor glanced at Donna and raised his eyebrows. 'Might have done. You inferring he was telling porkies?'

'Darac-7 is an opportunist, Doctor. He's a bounty hunter, a mercenary, a slave trader, an arms dealer and a pirate. He makes money however and wherever he can, and he doesn't care who he hurts in the process.'

'Is that right?' the Doctor said, as if he didn't believe a word.

'Is he telling the truth?' Donna hissed.

The Doctor gave a non-committal shrug.

Addressing Gopal, she said, 'If that's true, then what makes you think *we'd* be involved with a scumbag like that? I'm a bit insulted, as it goes. Do I *look* like the sort of person who hangs around with gangsters?'

'I cannot deny the evidence of my own eyes,' Gopal replied.

'What, all seven million of 'em?' Donna snapped back.

The Doctor gave her a mildly reproving look and asked, 'What evidence is that?'

'At the temple this morning you claimed that Darac-7's ship relocated when you attempted to penetrate its glamour with your sonic device. But I believe you used your sonic device to divert the ship to a location where the humans would not discover it. And this afternoon, at the Campbells' residence, you used your sonic device to summon Darac-7's gelem warriors. And now here you are, safely returned from your meeting with Darac-7. Why would he let you go unless you were in league with him?'

The Doctor shook his head, a half-smile on his face. 'I can see where you're coming from, Veec-9, me old chum, but you're wrong. First off, Darac-7 told me the ship in the temple was yours, not his. And second, this lovely little sonic of mine is brilliant at opening doors and detecting energy emissions and putting up shelves, but I can't relocate great big spaceships with it or whistle up my own personal posse of gelem warriors.

Here, have a look if you don't believe me.'

The Doctor flicked his arm up and suddenly the sonic was flipping end over end towards Gopal. Reacting instinctively, Gopal raised his left hand to catch it – but was distracted enough to lower his gun arm in order to do so. Immediately something flew out of nowhere and struck the back of his gun hand. Gopal cried out and his fingers sprang open. As soon as the gun started to fall, the Doctor was running towards the alien. He had reached Gopal and scooped the gun up from the dusty ground before Gopal had time to react.

It all happened so fast that Donna just stood there, dazed. She couldn't work out how the Doctor had made Gopal drop the gun until she saw Cameron appear round the corner of the wall at the end of the alleyway, holding his catapult.

'Where did you spring from?' she said.

Cameron looked a little shamefaced. 'I was in the house when the Doctor came back with those horrible ghost-men. I saw it all from an upstairs window. I wanted to know what was going on, so... I followed you.'

Donna shook her head. 'Your mum and dad aren't half gonna kill you, you know.'

'I'm sure you're right,' agreed Cameron. 'But I saved you and the Doctor from being shot. I reckon that's worth a beating.'

'Sorry to burst your bubble, but old Veec-9 here

wouldn't have shot us,' said the Doctor airily. 'As an evil intergalactic warlord, he's… well, a bit rubbish. Not that we're not grateful to you,' he added, winking at Cameron.

Donna looked at Gopal, who was rubbing the back of his hand and looking sorry for himself.

'Please, Doctor,' he whimpered, 'if you have an ounce of decency in your soul, kill me now.'

He looked so wretched that Donna couldn't help feeling sorry for him. 'Why do you want us to kill you?' she asked.

'I don't,' said Gopal, 'but a quick death is preferable to the slow torture that awaits me back on Jal Paloor.'

'Well, if you *will* build up an army and try to overthrow the government,' Donna said, rolling her eyes. 'We've got a saying here on Earth, chum – if you can't do the time, don't do the crime.'

'Ooh, harsh,' said the Doctor.

'My only crime was to speak out against the tyrants of the Hive Council,' Gopal replied. 'I made public my disapproval of the current regime, as a result of which my nucleus colony was destroyed and the Council placed a bounty on my head. I have been running for eleven quadrants. I made landfall here three cycles ago. I thought I was safe, I thought I had finally shaken off my pursuers. But once again Darac-7 has found me. After observing your actions today, I could only conclude that you were working in conjunction with him.'

'Yeah, well, we're not,' said the Doctor, 'and if you want my opinion, which most people do, I'd say we've all been hoodwinked. Not that I didn't have my suspicions, of course. Soon as I met Darac-7, I thought his eyes were too close together.' He held out his hand. 'Pass me my sonic, would you, Veec-9?'

Gopal looked down at his left hand, and seemed surprised to find he was still holding the Doctor's sonic screwdriver. Meekly he handed it over.

'Ta,' the Doctor said. He pressed the sonic to a hexagonal dial mounted on top of the thin tubular gun in his other hand and turned it on. After a moment he switched the sonic off and tossed the gun back to Gopal, who caught it in both hands, a startled expression on his face.

'There you go,' the Doctor said. 'I've melted the energy cells. Might as well chuck it away now – though it'd probably make a decent paperweight.'

Gopal looked at the gun in bemusement and then put it in his pocket. 'So… does this mean you are going to let me go?' he asked hopefully.

'Not only that,' said the Doctor, 'but we're going to put our heads together and think of a way of getting Darac-7 off your back for good. Where do you live, Veec-9? As a human, I mean?'

In something of a daze, Gopal gestured vaguely. 'I have an apartment a few streets from here.'

'Lovely,' said the Doctor. 'Nice splash of Darjeeling

and a cosy chat, I think.' He was striding away before anyone could respond. 'Well, come on, you lot,' he called back over his shoulder, 'chop-chop.'

Becharji was observing the preparations for dinner when he heard Mrs Campbell scream.

Snapping at the servants to continue their work, he hurried from the dining room. The scream had come from the drawing room directly across the wide hallway. As he strode across the wooden floor, he glimpsed movement to his left, and turned to see Ronny hurrying down the stairs in his shirtsleeves, drying his hands on a towel.

'Was that Mother?' Ronny asked, frowning.

Becharji bobbed his head. 'I believe so, sahib.'

The words were barely out of his mouth when the two of them heard Sir Edgar bark, 'Get back! Get back I say, or God help me, I'll run you through.'

Decorum forgotten, Ronny and Becharji made a dash for the drawing room. Just before they reached the door they heard the clatter of furniture falling over, accompanied by the shrill crash of breaking china.

Ronny reached out and yanked the door open. The sight that met his eyes stopped him momentarily in his tracks. His mother was cowering behind his father, who was armed with a poker and standing in a classic fencer's stance. Ronny knew that his rotund and bewhiskered father had not fenced since his Oxford

University days, and the sight of him standing there in his linen suit and highly polished shoes would have been comical had it not been for the two horrific creatures bearing down on him.

Ronny had been told all about the 'ghost-men' who had appeared in the garden that afternoon, having apparently materialised out of thin air. However, the second-hand accounts, no matter how vivid, had been unable to prepare him for quite *how* terrible the creatures were in the flesh.

They were not merely pale, as he had envisaged, but *white*. There was not even a tracery of veins beneath their marble-smooth skin, and neither did they possess wrinkles or hair, birthmarks or moles. Worst of all, the creatures had no eyes, and yet somehow they could *see*, or at least sense, the exact layout of the room and the position of everyone within it. They did not move with the blundering uncertainty of blind men, but with smooth and remorseless purpose.

The creatures had been advancing on Sir Edgar and Mary Campbell with outstretched hands, but as Ronny and Becharji burst into the room one of them swung back to confront the newcomers. Ronny faltered for a moment, such was the aura of malevolence that clung to the creature, and then he raised his fists in readiness for the fray. He had been a keen pugilist in his younger days and, thanks to his recent army experience, was still close to the peak of physical fitness.

Not knowing whether the creatures would understand or even hear him, he said loudly, 'Unless you gentlemen wish to receive a damn good thumping, I strongly advise you to leave this minute.'

'Hear, hear,' barked Sir Edgar with a warning jab of the poker.

But the creatures ignored Ronny's warning. They continued to advance, their hands outstretched like children playing blind man's buff.

Ronny threw his first punch at the same moment that his father lunged and thrust at his opponent's chest with the poker. In both instances, the outcome proved the same. Moving like lightning, the 'ghost-men' shot out their hands, one stopping Ronny's fist in mid-air as easily as if it was catching a ball, the other grabbing the poker and twisting it from Sir Edgar's grasp before tossing it almost disdainfully aside.

Becharji, hovering at Ronny's shoulder, was not entirely sure what happened next. He had not witnessed the incident in the garden that afternoon, but he had been told about it, and that was enough to make him realise that something similar was happening now. As he watched Ronny and his father begin to grapple with the intruders, the room suddenly filled with a strange silvery light. Becharji threw up his hand to shield his eyes as the light flared, and by the time it faded he found himself staring not at a knot of men engaged in hand-to-hand combat, but into the wide, shocked eyes of Lady Mary, who promptly gave a high-pitched sigh and fainted dead away.

'Can we trust him, Doctor?' Donna murmured.

Gopal was in the kitchen, making tea. The Doctor, Donna and Cameron were sitting in sagging wicker chairs in his modest apartment, a ceiling fan whizzing above their heads. The floor-length wooden shutters that led on to the balcony were standing open, beyond which they could see that a little of the sun's lustre was beginning to seep from the sky. Despite that it was still hot, almost sultry, like the atmosphere before a storm. The fan was doing little more than stir the warm air around.

The Doctor looked relaxed, long legs stretched out, hands behind his head. 'Yeah, I think so.'

'But how can you tell?' she persisted.

'His ears didn't turn blue.'

'What?'

'When Jal Karaths lie, their ears turn blue.' Then he jerked upright. 'No, hang on. That's the Fostarones. Silly me.'

'So he *could* be lying?' Donna said.

'Nah, course he's not lying. Blimey, you're suspicious. Doubting Donna they ought to call you. Doubting Donna from Dagenham.'

'I'm not *from* Dagenham,' she said.

'Yeah, well, you should be. Or Deptford. Or Dulwich.

Or Doncaster, that'd be a good one. Doubting Donna from Doncaster. Anyway, it's obvious he's not lying. He's got an honest face. And he's making tea. The Daleks have never made me tea. The Cybermen have never made me tea. The Sontarans never—'

'All right,' Donna shouted. She took a deep breath, then said it again, more calmly. 'All right, you've made your point. But I swear, if this tea's poisoned, I'll swing for you.'

The Doctor looked at Cameron, grimaced and raised his eyebrows. Cameron smiled back uncertainly.

They had been in Gopal's apartment – comparing notes, telling their respective stories – for over half an hour now.

Gopal had arrived on Earth three months earlier, and had been living among the humans ever since. His craft, smaller and sleeker than his pursuer's, and powered not by a leaking zytron core but by a self-generating fusion coil, was secreted in the centre of an inhospitable mountain range to the north of Calcutta, enclosed within a glamour shield that made it invisible to the human eye. In fact, Gopal told them, his glamour technology was far superior to that used by Darac-7. This was why he had been able to leave his ship and walk among the humans, whereas Darac-7 had had to rely on gelem warriors to do his dirty work for him.

When the Doctor called Gopal by his Jal Karath name, Veec-9, Gopal held up a hand.

'Please,' he said, 'I would be grateful if you would call me by my adopted name. In fact…' he hesitated.

'Go on,' the Doctor said softly, as if he knew what was coming.

'No doubt you'll think I'm foolish, Doctor, but I had been hoping that I might be able to stay here. To start a new life. As a human.'

'Well, you could do worse,' the Doctor said, glancing at Donna and flashing her a smile. 'I'm sure you'd be a great asset, Gopal.'

Now Gopal reappeared from his tiny kitchen, bearing a tray weighed down with a china teapot, four china cups and a plate of roughly cut yellow biscuits studded with raisins and cashew nuts.

'Lovely,' said the Doctor as Gopal put the tray down on a low wooden table. 'Shall I be mother?'

'I can't believe I'm drinking tea with two aliens and a little kid in India twenty years before I was born,' Donna muttered.

'I know,' said the Doctor, grinning all over his face. 'Brilliant, isn't it!'

When they were sat, sipping tea and crunching biscuits, Gopal said, 'I still don't understand why Darac-7 let you go so readily, Doctor.'

'Two reasons,' said the Doctor, his voice muffled through a mouthful of biscuit. 'Number one, he wanted to play the two of us off against one another. He couldn't find you, and he knew my technology was tons better than his, so he thought that if he filled me full of lies about you I'd rush out, track you down and deliver you into his evil clutches.'

He paused, holding up his hand. They all waited patiently for him to continue. However, he seemed, quite literally, to have bitten off more than he could chew. Finally Donna got fed up of waiting and said, 'And two, he wanted the TARDIS.'

The Doctor swallowed his biscuit. 'Aw, I was gonna say that.' Instantly he grabbed another biscuit and bit into it, waving it in the air with upraised eyebrows to express his admiration. Spraying crumbs, he continued, 'Not that it'll do him much good. He won't be able to open it. It'll just sit there in the corner of his ship like a big blue lemon, taking up space and gathering dust.'

'What—' Donna began, but then they heard the faint sound of chanting from outside. The chanting rapidly grew loud enough for them to make out the words: 'Long live the Father… long live the Father…'

The Doctor grinned. 'Sounds like the cavalry's arrived.' He jumped up and ran out onto the balcony.

The street was filled with people. As ever, Gandhi's appearance in public had attracted an ever-growing band of dedicated followers. The little man's familiar, white-clad figure was visible at the head of the chanting crowd. Next to Gandhi was Ranjit, who looked up at the Doctor's shouted greeting and saw him grinning and waving from the balcony.

'Mr Doctor! Mr Doctor!' Ranjit shouted, jumping up and down.

'Hang on, I'll come down and let you in,' the Doctor called. 'Don't think we'll have enough biscuits for all your mates, though.'

Three minutes later, Gandhi was settled in the chair that the Doctor had vacated for him, and Ranjit was sitting cross-legged on the floor, munching biscuits. The crowd below were still happily chanting away. The Doctor leaned against the wall, arms folded, one leg crossed in front of the other.

'How did you know where to find us?' Donna asked.

'We didn't,' said Ranjit. 'I knew Mr Gopal lived here because he brought me back earlier to give me some food before I returned to the camp.'

'The boy looked so thin,' Gopal explained, as if embarrassed by his generosity.

'And so I decided to ask him if he knew where Mr Doctor was.'

'And now you've found him,' Donna said.

'So what's happened?' asked the Doctor quietly.

'The half-made men came to the camp, Mr Doctor,' said Ranjit. 'Many, many of them. The people ran, but the half-made men still took them – just as they took you earlier. Whoosh, like that.'

The Doctor frowned, staring into space.

Donna asked, 'Why would they attack the camp, Doctor? Were they looking for Mohandas?'

The Doctor shook his head. 'As far as Darac-7's concerned, Mohandas is no different to any other human. No, they're harvesting. You said Darac-7 was an opportunist, Gopal. You're obviously not his only business interest – probably not even his main one.'

'What do you mean, "harvesting"?' Donna asked. 'That doesn't sound good.'

'I told you that the leaders of the eleven hives were corrupt,' said Gopal. 'There have been rumours on Jal Paloor for some time that the Hive Council has initiated a build-up of secret military forces on one of the outlying planets. It is said they are planning to spread across the stars, to establish a new and glorious empire. Of course, no one really believed it.'

'Except that it's true,' said the Doctor grimly, 'and they're going to use gelem warriors to do it.'

'So as well as looking for Gopal, this Darac bloke is kidnapping humans to sell to the Hive Council to make into them gelem things?' said Donna.

The Doctor nodded.

'And he's keeping 'em… where? You said his spaceship was pretty poky. So are all those people being transported straight to the planet of the weeds or what? No offence, Gopal.'

The Doctor stared at Donna. Then he marched across the room, grabbed her shoulders and pulled her to him in a fierce hug.

'Brilliant!' he shouted.

'What did I—' she began, but the Doctor was already off, running his hands through his hair and talking at a hundred miles an hour.

'If he's taking this many people, he must have a holding area close to his ship. Somewhere huge and out of sight – an underground cavern, maybe. When he's reaped his first harvest he'll give his mates on the Hive Council a bell and they'll send a prison ship to pick up the first consignment. The gelem warriors he's already using must be programmed to transmit straight into the holding area with every new catch and then back out again. So if we can get those coordinates…' He looked up wildly. 'Gopal, how do you move to and fro between here and your ship? Transmat pod?'

Gopal nodded.

'Mind if I have a look at it?'

'Certainly, Doctor,' said Gopal. 'Would you help me move this table?'

Gopal and the Doctor lifted aside the low table on which the tea things stood and placed it against the wall. Beneath the table was a red and green rug, which Gopal rolled up, revealing a neat, hinged square in the wooden floor. He produced a key, unlocked the trapdoor and raised it. In the gap between the joists was a small hidey-hole.

Donna caught a glimpse of various neatly stacked

alien artefacts – *boys' toys*, she thought. There were things made of brushed black metal, studded with dials and switches and flickering green lights. Gopal extracted a device like a miniature rugby ball, which he handed to the Doctor.

'Ooh, nice,' the Doctor said.

He took a moment to familiarise himself with the array of controls set into the top of the device, then produced his sonic and pressed its glowing blue tip to different parts of the device, hmming and ahing as he did so.

Finally he switched the sonic off and grinned at them. He was about to speak when the air shimmered in the centre of the room.

Next moment, four gelem warriors were standing there in a diamond formation, their backs to each other, facing outward. Instantly they raised their hands and began to advance on the room's six occupants.

Donna tried to make a break for the door, but the gelem warrior closest to it was too quick for her. She changed direction, and backed towards the open doors leading on to the balcony, wondering whether she'd be able to jump to the ground below without breaking any bones.

Out of the corner of her eye she saw everyone else taking evasive action – everyone except Gandhi. As the Doctor pressed himself up against the wall and the boys dived behind items of furniture, Gandhi simply sat in his chair, refusing either to fight back or run away. Donna saw him looking up with an expression of serene curiosity as a gelem warrior reached out for him.

TWELVE

The cavern was vast and stifling, condensation dripping from the roof. Aside from a few small fires, the makeshift prison was lit only by a red, crackling barrier, which encircled the hundreds of people clustered within it. Already Adelaide had seen one man stretch out a hand to the barrier, only to be blasted unconscious for his trouble. She scanned the dirty, sweaty faces of her fellow captives, some of whom were weeping in fear, some stunned with shock, some simply staring resignedly into space, and wondered whether she was in Hell.

How long she had been here she wasn't sure. It seemed like for ever, but was probably no more than a couple of hours. At frequent intervals, the air would shimmer and the chalk-men would appear with more captives. Together with Edward, Adelaide had taken it upon herself to try and reassure these often terrified and confused people, acclimatise them to their new surroundings. It was exhausting work, but by keeping busy she was at least able to prevent herself from indulging in her own fearful thoughts.

She was trying to calm a little girl, who had been separated from her parents at the camp and was wailing in fear, when a voice called, 'Adelaide? Is that you?'

She looked over her shoulder, and to her joy and despair, saw Ronny making his way through the throng towards her. He was dressed for dinner, but his white shirt was streaked with sweat and grime, and he had a smudge of dirt on his cheek. His stiff collar and neatly knotted tie looked incongruous, almost comical, in these surroundings.

Adelaide jumped to her feet and flung her arms around him. 'Oh, Ronny!' she cried. 'Not you too!'

'Afraid so,' Ronny said. 'Can you believe, those awful creatures actually came in to the house? The sheer cheek of it!'

'Who else—' Adelaide began, and then over Ronny's shoulder she saw her father and mother and a solicitous Becharji trying to struggle their way through the grimy mass of humanity.

'Oh no,' she cried despairingly, 'not *all* of you.'

'All but Cameron, I'm afraid,' said Ronny. 'First the blighters took Father and I, then they had the gall to go back for Mother and Becharji.'

'My dear Adelaide,' Sir Edgar said, and with an uncharacteristic show of affection gave his daughter a hug. 'Ronny said he'd spotted you. I told him he was seeing things.' He mopped his brow with a grubby handkerchief. 'What is this hellish place?'

'Not a clue,' Adelaide said. 'Are you all right, Mother?'

Mary Campbell had a lace handkerchief pressed to her nose and a look of distaste on her tearful face.

'What a silly question,' she said in a shrill, strained voice. 'Of *course* I'm not all right. How *can* I be all right, crammed into this appalling place with all these… these *people*.'

Suddenly all the fear, confusion and anxiety of the last few hours rose up in Adelaide and came bubbling out of her.

'Is that all you can find to worry about, Mother?' she snapped. 'The fact that you've been forced to mix with people you consider below your social standing? Because, like it or not, we're all in this together. We're all living, thinking, feeling human beings – and we're *all* scared.'

There was an uncomfortable silence, and then, quite unexpectedly, her father nodded.

'Quite right, my dear,' he said gruffly, and patted her shoulder. 'Quite right.'

***

As Donna pressed herself back against the wall, she was vaguely aware of the Doctor stepping forward, the rugby ball device in his upraised hand. He fiddled with it for a second, and suddenly crackling tendrils of yellow-white light erupted out of it.

Like jittering electric serpents, the tendrils of light sought out the gelem warriors. Donna watched as one tendril latched on to the centre of the chest of the creature menacing her and formed the fizzing outline of a circle. Immediately, all four warriors began to jerk and spasm, like a group of men struck by the same bolt of lightning. They twitched grotesquely for a few moments, and then simply keeled over, as stiff and expressionless as mannequins.

The Doctor switched the device off. For a second, nobody moved.

Then Ranjit asked, 'Are the half-made men dead?'

'They were never really alive,' the Doctor replied, and absently tossed the rugby ball device across to Gopal. He produced his sonic screwdriver again and held it up. 'Better tweak the frequency on this. It's like a homing beacon for them.' He fiddled with the controls for a moment. 'There we go. That should fool 'em for a bit.' He dropped to his knees beside one of the lifeless forms, pressed the sonic to its chest and turned it on.

To everyone's amazement there was a hissing noise and a circle of rubbery white flesh rose and swivelled on a sort of flap. Nestled within a cavity beneath was a flattish silver disc, shimmering with light, that reminded Donna of a hockey puck. Another zap of the sonic and a trio of claw-like metal catches sprang open, enabling the Doctor to reach in and free the disc from its housing.

'What's that?' asked Cameron. 'Its heart?'

'Matter relocator,' said the Doctor.

'Didn't you say the coordinates on that would take us straight into the holding area?' said Donna.

The Doctor nodded and turned on his sonic again. 'But if I make a slight adjustment…' He tinkered for a moment, then sat back. 'Job's a good 'un. All aboard who are coming aboard.'

They all looked at each other. Donna said, 'You're not going without me, sunshine,' and grabbed the Doctor's arm.

Gopal took Donna's hand. 'And I cannot allow you to fight my battles for me.'

Gandhi too rose from his seat. 'Curiosity is a terrible curse,' he said sadly. 'I really should not give in to it.' Then he smiled, and grasped Gopal's other hand.

'If you're going, Bapu, I am coming too,' cried Ranjit, and attached himself to the human chain.

Cameron looked terrified, but he grabbed his friend's arm. 'I'm not going to be the only one left behind,' he said.

The Doctor grinned, as if they were about to embark on the most thrilling funfair ride ever.

'Stand clear of the doors!' he bellowed. 'Here we go!'

Cameron was aware of a sickening sideways lurch as the room dissolved around him. There was a horrible sensation of his surroundings rushing by at such speed that it was impossible to focus upon a single detail. His stomach rolling with nausea, he closed his eyes and clung tightly to Ranjit's hand. He dreaded to think what would happen if he let go.

'We're here.'

The Doctor's voice popped the build-up of pressure in his ears. Cameron couldn't believe how cheerful the Doctor sounded. He opened his eyes to find himself standing on a rocky slope leading up to a craggy range of hills. The sky above was deepening towards dusk, but it was not yet too dark for Cameron to make out the cave openings that punctured the forbidding mass of bare and jagged rock above them. Some of the openings were taller than a man, whereas others might have proved a tight squeeze for a rabbit, or even a snake. Beyond each of the cave openings Cameron could see nothing but blackness.

'That was rough,' Donna said. She was leaning forward, hands on knees. 'Dunno about you lot, but I think I'm gonna hurl.'

'Deep breaths,' the Doctor said. He held up the sonic and frowned. 'Though on the other hand…'

'What is it, Doctor?' Gopal asked.

'This whole area is steeped in zytron energy. The leakage is getting worse. Though on the plus side, it'll make Darac-7 easier to find. Come on, let's not hang about.'

He strode up the slope as if out for an afternoon yomp. Gopal and the boys hurried after him.

'You all right, Mohandas?' Donna asked.

Gandhi was looking around at the barren landscape, eyes gleaming like an excited child's. 'Oh yes,' he breathed. 'I am struck with wonder.'

'You get used to it after a while,' Donna said, and then realised that the throwaway remark was not really how she felt. She linked arms with the little man. 'Actually, you don't. You never get used to it. That's why it's so amazing. Before I met the Doctor, I never realised there was so much to see.'

'Come on, you two!'

The Doctor had already reached the top of the slope. 'What you doing?' he called. 'Having a picnic?'

Donna rolled her eyes at Gandhi and together they hurried up the slope. By the time they reached the Doctor, she was gasping for breath, but Gandhi seemed as fresh as ever. Not for the first time, she was struck by how spry and sinewy the little man was.

'We're not all descended from mountain goats, you know,' she said, trying not to pant.

'No, not like on Istervaal,' the Doctor replied

absently. 'Evolution didn't half take a funny old turn there.' Abruptly he clapped his hands, like a teacher on a field trip. 'Right, gang, here's the plan. Once we're inside, we've got four objectives. One, put a stop to Darac-7 – but leave that to me, I'm brilliant at that sort of thing; two, find the holding cells and release the prisoners; three, keep an eye out for a big blue box, cos that's my TARDIS and it might turn out to be our only way out; and four, back home in time for tea and crumpets. Everybody happy with that? T'riffic. Off we go.'

He led the way forward, and marched without hesitation into one of the larger cave openings. In his right hand he brandished the sonic, which glowed like a tiny torch, bathing the rocky walls in cold blue light.

For the next fifteen minutes, the motley group moved through the narrow tunnels, the Doctor leading the way like a tour guide. They progressed mostly in silence, though occasionally the Doctor would mutter, 'This way,' or 'Left here.' At one point there was a clunk and the Doctor looked round at them, rubbing his head. 'Careful,' he said ruefully, 'the roof's a bit low just here.'

A couple of minutes later he said, 'Whoa,' and came to an abrupt halt, spreading his arms.

Donna was just behind him. She stood on tiptoe to peer over his shoulder. 'What is it?'

Then they heard it – a rapid, intermittent scuttling from the darkness ahead. Cautiously the Doctor extended the sonic, but the blue light couldn't stretch more than a few feet.

'Hang on,' he said, and next moment he had a pencil-torch in his hand. He turned it on and shone it into the pitch-black tunnel.

'Oh my God,' breathed Donna.

In the narrow passage, less than three metres away, were three scorpions. They were each the size of small dogs, each twisted and deformed and covered in blackish lumps. One was crouched on the ground, legs wide apart as though readying itself to spring, and the other two were clinging to the right-hand wall.

As though angered by the light, the scorpion on the ground extended its claws and hissed like a snake, raising itself on its misshapen legs and swaying from side to side.

'Cover your ears,' the Doctor muttered, and adjusted the controls on the sonic. Immediately it made a hideous screeching sound. Donna clapped her hands over her ears, feeling as though someone was drilling into the top of her skull. The walls of the tunnel seemed to shake. Dust sifted from the ceiling.

The Doctor strode forward, teeth gritted, sonic held at arm's length. The scorpion on the ground reared up on its back legs, body quivering. It looked for a moment as though it was being physically repelled by the terrible sound, and then it turned and scuttled into the darkness.

Moving awkwardly, hampered by their zytron-distorted bodies, the other scorpions scrambled away too, disappearing into crevices in the walls.

The Doctor readjusted the sonic so that it was once more warbling at its usual level. He pulled a series of faces, as if testing the elasticity of his skin. 'Well, that's one way of clearing your sinuses,' he said.

They moved forward again, the group behind the Doctor clustered more closely together now, their heads darting left and right, as if imagining all kinds of scuttling monstrosities in the shadows.

Abruptly the Doctor came to a halt in front of a blank section of stone wall.

'Why have we stopped now?' Donna asked nervously.

'We're here,' the Doctor said.

'Where's here?'

He turned and grinned at the others, his face a deathly blue mask in the light from the sonic. 'You'll like this,' he said.

He touched the sonic to the wall and instantly the rock transformed into a porthole-like opening, which seemed to be composed of the spiky, overlapping petals of some exotic flower.

'What's that?' gasped Cameron.

'That,' said the Doctor grandly, 'is the door to an alien spaceship.'

'Are we going inside?' Ranjit breathed, eyes wide.

'Some of us are,' the Doctor said.

It was decided that the Doctor, Gandhi and Ranjit would enter the ship, whilst Donna, Gopal and Cameron would try to find and free the prisoners. The Doctor sonicked the now-exposed door of the ship, the boys gasping and Gandhi clapping his hands in wonder as the 'petals' folded smoothly back, revealing a gleaming black chamber full of thick loops of cable and shiny tangles of machinery.

The Doctor fiddled with the sonic until it began to make a slow but steady beeping sound, then handed it to Donna. 'The prisoners will be somewhere in this cave system,' he said, 'within a stasis barrier contained behind a glamour shield. The sonic has been tuned in to pick up the energy emissions. It'll beep faster the closer you get, slower if you start moving away. When the beeps become a continuous noise you'll know you're there.'

'Then what?' Donna asked.

'Then you turn it to setting 59-A. That should get you in. Oh, and you'd better have these.' He gave her the torch and the matter relocator he had taken from the gelem warrior's chest. 'You might need an alternative escape route. The relocator will take you back out onto the slope where we came in.'

'What about you?' she asked.

'I'll have the TARDIS. Hopefully. See you in a bit.'

'Good luck,' she said, giving him a hug.

He clicked his tongue and winked at her. 'You make your own luck in this game.'

'I think this is it,' Donna said.

The journey through the caves had been tense but uneventful. Once or twice they had heard scuffling movements in the darkness, but they hadn't seen anything. It had been easy to follow the signal of the sonic. Each time they came to a fork they simply took one turn or the other and listened to the beeps. If the beeps sped up, they knew they were on the right track. If they slowed down, they retraced their steps and took the alternative route.

It had taken twenty minutes of tramping through stifling darkness before the beeps turned into what Donna would have described as a continuous note. She stopped and looked around. They appeared to be nowhere special. There were rocky walls on either side and a craggy ceiling a couple of metres above their heads. She turned the sonic to setting 59-A, as the Doctor had instructed, and touched it against the left-hand wall. When nothing happened she walked across to the right-hand wall and tried again. Instantly the wall shimmered and disappeared.

In front of them was a wide black tunnel sloping downwards over jagged rocks.

'Is it just me or is there a red glow ahead?' she asked.

Gopal nodded.

'It looks like a fire,' said Cameron.

Donna switched off the sonic and turned on the torch. 'Everyone OK?' she asked.

Gopal and Cameron nodded.

'Come on then.'

They made their way down over the large, jagged rocks, which formed a series of natural shelves and plateaus. Donna felt like a mouse negotiating a giant, crumbling staircase. The red glow grew brighter as they descended, so much so that Donna turned off the torch and put it back in her pocket. As they drew closer, they realised that the red glow was also accompanied by a crackling and humming, like the sound made by the wires linking electricity pylons on a rainy day.

Eventually the slope levelled out and the tunnel narrowed slightly. The three of them moved cautiously forward, the crackling red glow now filling the arch ahead.

It wasn't until they were standing under the arch itself that the view opened out before them. It was like walking along a cliff-top and not being able to see the crashing waves below until you went right up to the edge and peered over.

Donna gasped. Below her was a cavern the size of a football stadium. It was surrounded by a fiercely crackling red barrier, and it was filled with people – hundreds, perhaps thousands of people. Most of them were huddled silently together in groups. Some were clustered around meagre fires that they had somehow managed to light. Donna looked around at the array of red-lit faces and saw shock, fear, dejection.

In a bitter voice Gopal said, 'When the cave is full, Darac-7 will ship these people to where the Hive Council are creating their secret army, and then he will use his gelem warriors to harvest more. As long as the Hive Council keep paying him, the harvest will continue.'

Donna thought of the way the Ood had been treated on the Ood-Sphere. This was just as sickening. She was about to say so when Cameron cried, 'I can see Mother and Father and Becharji! And Ronny and Adelaide! Look!'

He was pointing to the right, almost jumping up and down in his excitement. Even amongst all these people, the Campbells were not too difficult to spot. They were standing in a close-knit group, whereas almost everyone else was sitting, added to which they were dressed differently to most of the people around them.

Cameron's high-pitched voice must have carried down to the cavern below, because all at once Donna saw people looking up, pointing at them. The low buzz of chatter, barely discernible before above the crackling hum of the barrier, now rose in volume as news of their presence spread through the crowd.

'We've been spotted,' Donna said. 'We'd better go and let 'em all out before they start thinking we're the ones who trapped 'em here.'

They picked their way down the final rubbly slope to the base of the cavern. There was a surge in the crowd as people moved forward to meet them.

Word must have filtered back to the Campbells that Cameron was there because, by the time they reached the bottom of the slope, Ronny was shouldering his way to the front of the crowd, closely followed by Adelaide, his parents and Becharji.

'What in Heaven's name are *you* doing here?' Ronny asked in astonishment.

Cameron grinned. 'We're rescuing you.'

'Stand back,' Donna said, holding up the sonic. 'This thing's loaded.'

Hoping that setting 59-A would work not only on the glamour but on the barrier too, she stepped as close as she dared and pointed the sonic at it. The crowd drew back, murmuring concernedly as the activity of the barrier seemed momentarily to increase. Donna gritted her teeth as red sparks flew in all directions, fizzing like angry sprites. Then ragged holes appeared in the barrier, until suddenly, with a final furious crackle, it collapsed.

There was a moment of shocked disbelief as — aside from a little firelight and the glow of the sonic — the cavern was plunged into darkness. Then people began to cheer and whoop and wave their hands in the air. Donna turned the sonic off as Ronny stepped forward.

'Miss Donna, I could hug you,' he exclaimed.

She sized him up. He was a good-looking bloke. 'Well, don't let me stop you,' she said.

Suddenly she was surrounded by people grinning and slapping her on the back. Already some were streaming up the rocky slope towards the arch above, intent on finding a way out. Some were lighting matches to see by, others grabbing glowing bits of wood from the fires. Despite the near-darkness and the fact that most of them probably didn't have a clue where they were, the mood was one of jubilation at suddenly finding themselves free.

Adelaide had lifted Cameron up and was spinning him around, laughing. Sir Edgar, Mary and Ronny were bombarding Donna with questions.

Suddenly the air in the cavern shimmered in a dozen different places, and people began to panic as gelem warriors appeared in their midst. All at once there were people running in all directions. Many of them slipped and fell, tripping over rocks in the semi-darkness, or knocked over in the rush to escape.

The gelem warriors waded forward, swinging their arms, ripping and tearing with their hands. Evidently the disabling of the barrier had been detected.

'Come on,' Donna said, herding the Campbells

before her. 'Leg it.'

They joined the throng of people scrambling up the rocky slope towards the arch above. Almost immediately, however, it became obvious that Sir Edgar and his wife, unused to physical exertion, were moving too slowly to escape the clutches of the advancing gelem warriors. Much as she loathed the thought of leaving all the freed prisoners to fend for themselves, Donna held up the matter relocator the Doctor had given her. 'We'll have to use this,' she shouted to Gopal.

'Not yet,' he said. 'I have this.' He produced the transmat pod which the Doctor had altered with his sonic. He placed it on the ground, twisted something on top of the device and crackling threads of yellow-white light suddenly leaped from an aperture in the top. Remembering what had happened earlier, Donna hastily placed the matter relocator she was holding on a nearby rock. Although the Doctor had reconfigured the settings on this particular device, she didn't want to risk getting zapped like the gelem warriors in Gopal's apartment had done.

Just as before, the tendrils of light sought out the matter relocator discs in the centre of the gelem warriors' chests. As the light hit them, the warriors began to jerk and shudder before crashing lifeless to the floor. Although Donna knew that the creatures were not in any real sense alive, it was still disturbing to watch them keel over and die.

Eventually Gopal switched off the device and nodded at the unaffected disc sitting on the rock. 'Now we can use the matter relocator to get out of here,' he said.

Donna looked down into the cavern. Most people were scrambling up the slope towards the arch now, or streaming through the tunnels in search of the openings that led out on to the hillside, but there were still several dozen people down below, who had either been battered unconscious by the gelem warriors or were too badly injured to move.

'I'm not leaving anybody behind,' she said.

Gopal nodded. 'You are right, of course. But we don't know how many people the matter relocator will carry.'

'Then let's find out,' she said.

'What will you do when you find the creature, Mr Doctor?' Ranjit whispered. 'Will you kill it?'

The Doctor looked disapproving. 'Course not. You can't go through life killing things just cos you don't agree with them. Isn't that right, Mohandas?'

Gandhi nodded. 'Violence solves nothing. Even when it seems to do good, the benefit is only temporary, whereas the evil it does is permanent.'

'There you go,' said the Doctor. 'Couldn't have put it better myself.'

'So what will you do, Mr Doctor?' Ranjit asked.

'Jaw-jaw not war-war.'

Ranjit shook his head. 'I don't understand.'

'I'll *talk* to it,' the Doctor said. 'We'll have a nice sit down and a little chat. Always the best way.'

'And if it does not listen?'

'I'll *make* it listen. I'll talk until it does. I'm good at talking. Never stop once I get going. Jabber jabber jabber, that's me. I'll tell you this, Ranjit, by the time I'm done, it'll be *begging* me to let it put right what it's done, just to shut me up. Here we are.'

He stopped abruptly in front of another petal-like opening. He raised a hand to knock, but before he could do so the 'petals' folded back. 'Looks like we're expected,' the Doctor said. 'Normally I'd say "after you", but you'd better let me go first.'

He stepped into the opening and strode along the short, throat-like corridor ahead. Ranjit followed, goggling at his surroundings, still overcome by the sheer wonder of the alien craft. He found it hard to believe that he was actually *inside* the ball of light which had fallen from the sky over a week ago. Although everything was made of strange metals and some kind of shiny rubber, he was reminded of both a thick jungle and the belly of some great fish which had swallowed them whole.

He followed the Doctor into an oddly shaped room, full of more of the rubbery vines and incredible machinery. His mouth dropped open when he saw that in the centre of the room, suspended like a spider in its web, was a huge black plant with hundreds of blinking eyes. Unable to speak, Ranjit looked at Gandhi, and was astonished to see that he was staring up at the plant with clasped hands, a rapt expression on his face. There were even tears glinting in his eyes, as if the horrible creature was the most beautiful sight he had ever seen.

The Doctor didn't even seem to notice the plant-creature at first. He walked over to a blue box on the left-hand side of the room and patted it like a pet dog. 'Hello, gorgeous,' he said, and then he spun round, strode up to the plant and pointed a finger at it.

'As for *you*, sunny Jim, you're a sneak and a liar, and you owe me a big fat apology.' He folded his arms and scowled. Two seconds passed. 'Well, come on, I'm waiting.'

Ranjit's eyes opened wide as an icy, high-pitched voice filled the room. 'You were foolish to come back here, Doctor.'

'Yeah, yeah, people are always telling me that,' the Doctor said. 'Did you honestly think, Darac-7, that I'd just sit back and let you carry on helping yourself to members of the human race as if they were sweets on a pick 'n' mix stand? Cos that's so not gonna happen. Instead what you're gonna do is power up those nasty little zytron engines of yours and vamoose out of here. And don't think about starting up your filthy little racket elsewhere, cos I'm gonna see to it that the whole base of operations is found, closed down and the extraction factories dismantled. If I were you, I'd find a nice quiet planet somewhere and keep your head low for a while. Right, I'll give you one hour to pack up and go. First and last chance. See ya.'

He turned and strode away without waiting for an answer. However, he had taken no more than half a dozen steps when the air in front of the circular exit shimmered and a gelem warrior appeared, blocking his path. Almost immediately the air shimmered again, and four more gelem warriors materialised, two on either side of Gandhi and Ranjit, cutting off every avenue of escape. The Doctor sighed, as if this was no more than a minor irritation. He spun on his heel and approached the Jal Karath again.

'You really don't want to mess with me, Darac-7,' he said grimly. 'If you listen to what your pulse sensors are saying, you'll know that your plans are already in ruins. Your first consignment of human fodder is halfway back to Calcutta by now. We've penetrated your glamour, dismantled your stasis barrier and disabled half your precious workforce. Believe me, your best bet is to leave and never come back. You win some, you lose some. Why not just put this one down to experience, eh?'

Once again the icy voice of the Jal Karath filled the air. 'I know that what you're telling me is true, Doctor, but I'm afraid that I don't accept defeat so easily. I'm a Hive-7 Jal Karath. We are the proudest and most patriotic of the eleven Hives. Unfortunately for you, that also makes us the most unforgiving.'

As if at some unspoken command, three of the gelem warriors lurched forward and grabbed the Doctor, Gandhi and Ranjit. Ranjit struggled fiercely, to no avail, but the Doctor and Gandhi remained still.

'Big mistake, Darac-7,' said the Doctor in a low voice.

'The mistake was yours, Doctor, by coming here. Now I'll have to create more gelem warriors and start the harvest all over again. But you can help me take the first step.'

Ranjit was still struggling, but the gelem warrior held him in an iron grip. 'What is he going to do with us, Mr Doctor?' he wailed.

As if in reply, a panel slid open in the back wall, to reveal an open-fronted cabinet-like device. The cabinet thrummed into life, lights flickering through a tubular system of inner workings. The Doctor's face twisted into an expression of abhorrence.

'What is that contrivance, Doctor?' Gandhi asked, his voice calm and steady.

'It's a extraction machine,' said the Doctor. He glared up at the Jal Karath. 'You can't do this, Darac-7.'

There was a peculiar bubbling sound – the sound of alien laughter. 'Oh, I think I can, Doctor. As you will imminently find out.'

'No,' the Doctor said, speaking quickly now, 'you don't understand. You really *can't* do this. Listen to me, Darac-7. You wanted to know what species I was? I'm a Time Lord. The *last* of the Time Lords. The only survivor of the Last Great Time War. And as a Time Lord I'm telling you that you *can't* put Mohandas Gandhi into that filthy machine. If you do, you'll tear the timelines apart. You'll plunge this planet, this whole galaxy, into a new Dark Age.'

There was a pause. Ranjit stared at the Doctor wide-eyed.

Finally Darac-7 murmured, 'Is that so?'

'Yes,' said the Doctor firmly, 'it is. So here's what I'll do. I'll make a deal with you. Take me. Take the boy even. But spare Gandhi. For the sake of the planet, *let him go.*'

There was a long pause. Then the Jal Karath said, 'No.'

The Doctor's eyes widened. 'What do you mean, "no"?'

'I mean no, Doctor. I will not accept your terms. What do I care if this galaxy is torn apart?'

'But... you'll be caught up in it,' the Doctor said desperately. 'You'll die along with everyone else.'

'I'm not an idiot, Doctor. We both know that the effects of the time disruption will not be felt immediately. It will spiral slowly down through the causal nexus, unravelling history as it goes. By the time it impacts on this axis point I will be long gone.'

'But… your harvest. Your precious warrior army.'

The quivering motion that rippled through the weed-like body of the Jal Karath was the equivalent of a shrug. 'There are other worlds, other galaxies. Millions of them.' Raising its voice it said, 'Place the old man in the machine.'

'No!' the Doctor yelled, struggling wildly. 'No, Darac-7, you *can't!*'

'Don't concern yourself, Doctor,' said Gandhi as he was led, unresisting, to the cabinet at the back of the room. 'I am not afraid to die. Fear of death makes us devoid of valour and faith.'

'But you're not meant to die *now*,' said the Doctor, still struggling hopelessly.

Gandhi smiled. 'If God says I am, then I am. Everything is in His hands.'

THIRTEEN

Gandhi walked across the room, his back straight and his head held high, and stepped into the machine. His face remained serene as levered metal arms swung inwards from each of the four corners of the cabinet and clamped together in the centre, sealing him in. Instantly, with a rising whine like an accelerating engine, the machine powered up, coloured lights beginning to flow over Gandhi's white-clad form. The Doctor slumped in his captive's immovable grip, his hair flopping over his face as his head drooped forward.

The high-pitched whine of the extraction machine climbed and climbed, building to an ear-splitting crescendo… and then suddenly there was a loud bang. A huge shower of sparks erupted out of the top of the cabinet, followed by a thick black cloud of smoke. The machine itself began to judder, the high-pitched whine to deepen and die as the power seeped away. Inside the machine, apparently unharmed, Gandhi looked around with an expression of mild interest.

The Jal Karath started to thrash and writhe in its web of technology. 'What's happening?' it screamed. 'I feel... *pain*.'

As though their command link had been cut off, the gelem warriors suddenly released the Doctor and Ranjit and stood motionless, their hands dropping to their sides.

Slowly the Doctor straightened up and raised his head. There was a grim, knowing look on his face.

'Thought that might happen,' he said quietly. 'I did warn you, Darac-7.'

Whatever fault had caused the extraction machine to overload now seemed to be having a knock-on effect on the rest of the ship's systems. Things were sparking and burning-out all over the place. Thick black smoke was filling the room.

'What did you do, Mr Doctor?' Ranjit asked, ducking as a shower of sparks burst from what looked like a melting metal box close to his head.

'Me? Nothing,' said the Doctor. 'It was Mohandas. He's just too good.'

The levered arms which had clamped Gandhi into the machine now sprang apart, releasing him. Stepping out, he overheard the Doctor's words. 'Good in what sense, Doctor?'

The Doctor was already darting from one of the ship's failing systems to another, apparently looking for something. Suddenly he exclaimed, 'Aha. You know what this is?'

Both Gandhi and Ranjit shook their heads.

'It's an energy inversion module. And if I just refine the search parameters and set it at maximum…' His fingers danced over an array of complex-looking controls, then he stepped back with a satisfied grin. His head whipped round and he stared at Gandhi. 'Sorry, what were you saying?'

'You said Bapu was too good, Mr Doctor,' Ranjit reminded him.

'Oh yeah, he is. Too good, too nice, too pure of heart. You see, the extraction machine works by sucking all the badness out of people, like the juice from a lemon, and storing it to be used later. But now and again someone comes along who hasn't got any badness in them – a genetic anomaly, or just someone with such incredible strength of mind that they've literally willed it away. When that happens – and we're talking… ooh, one out of every billion people here – the machine can't cope. It's like trying to boil a kettle with no water in it. Only problem for Darac-7 is that his kettle is linked to every other kitchen appliance, which in turn are linked to him…'

They ducked as an almighty explosion to their right scattered burning debris across a wide area. The Jal Karath screamed in pain.

'… and I'm afraid that his warranty has just run out,' concluded the Doctor. 'Follow me.'

With the alien craft collapsing in flames around them, the Doctor ran across to the TARDIS. He unlocked the door, bundled Gandhi and Ranjit ahead of him, and then leaped inside, slamming the door.

'Everybody ready?' Donna shouted.

She was at the centre of a massive human chain. Together with Gopal, Becharji, the Campbells and Adelaide's friend Edward Morgan, she had descended again to the cavern, issuing instructions to gather the unconscious and injured together into one area.

Gopal looked around to make sure everyone was in physical contact with the person beside them. He himself was holding the hand of an unconscious woman, whose other hand, in turn, was being held by a bewildered-looking man with a gash on his forehead. As far as he could see there were no breaks in the chain.

'We are ready here, Donna,' he called back.

'Here too,' Adelaide confirmed from the other side of the chain.

'Mr C?' Donna shouted, knowing that Sir Edgar's link of the chain was behind her, stretching from him to Cameron, who was clinging to her elbow as if his life depended on it.

'What? Oh yes,' he called in his bluff tones. He sounded as if he was actually enjoying himself. 'Chocks away!'

'Please, Edgar,' his wife said stiffly, 'can't you just—'

'Right, hold on tight everybody,' Donna yelled, taking some satisfaction from drowning out Mary Campbell's wheedling voice. 'Here we go!'

Trapped in its disintegrating web, the Jal Karath was contorted in agony.

'Doctor!' it screamed as the TARDIS faded away. 'Doctor, come back! Have pityyyy!'

Its dying plea blended with the rising screech of its critically overloading systems, becoming a final drawn-out howl.

Ranjit promptly fell to his knees, an expression of shock on his face. Gandhi, on the other hand, looked around the TARDIS in utter delight.

'Tell me, Doctor,' he said, 'is this box of yours alive?'

The Doctor was rushing round the console, twiddling dials, pulling levers and prodding buttons. He halted abruptly and looked over the console at Gandhi with something like admiration. 'Why do you ask?'

'Because it reminds me of the human brain. It

appears small and unimpressive on the outside, and yet it holds such wonders within.'

The Doctor's face broke into an enormous grin. 'You're incredible, you know that?' he said.

'Private Wilkins, sir.'

'Yes, Private Wilkins?' said Samuels, the Regimental Medical Officer. 'What can I do for you?'

'I just wondered how Major Daker was, sir? The lads are... well, we're worried about him.'

Samuels nodded curtly, looking up at the young Private from behind his desk. 'I'm sure the Major will appreciate your concern, Private. Naturally we're doing all we can for him, but as yet there's been no change in his condition.'

As if on cue, a furious shout suddenly came from the sick bay at the end of the corridor, shattering the early evening quiet.

'What the hell's going on? Why am I tied up like this?'

Wilkins looked at Samuels. 'It sounds to me as if the Major is back to his old self, sir.'

Samuels jumped up from his chair, rounded his desk and ran down the corridor. Wilkins hurried after him.

The sick bay was like a smaller version of the barracks in which the men slept – a row of four beds on either side of the room, separated by a narrow central aisle. Only one of the beds was presently occupied. As

Samuels burst into the room with Wilkins in tow, the patient raised his head.

Wilkins saw that the Major was indeed back to his old self. When they had brought him in earlier he had been covered in awful black lumps and had been raving and slavering like an animal. Now the lumps had miraculously disappeared, and he was looking alert and… well, *human* again.

The only thing that didn't seem to have improved was the Major's notorious temper.

'Samuels,' he barked, straining at the bonds with which the medical staff had been forced to restrain him, 'untie me at once. This is an outrage!'

As Samuels hurried forward to comply, a hideous trumpeting sound filled the room. Wilkins looked round wildly, wondering if a herd of crazed elephants was about to crash through the wall. A warm breeze suddenly kicked up from nowhere, ruffling the men's hair. As all three of them looked on in astonishment, Daker straining to raise himself from the bed to which he was secured, a tall blue box emblazoned with the word POLICE appeared out of thin air.

There was a moment of utter gaping disbelief, and then the door of the box opened and a skinny man wearing a blue suit emerged. The man looked around with keen interest. 'Hello, I'm the Doctor,' he said. 'Where's this then? Sick bay?'

Both Wilkins and Samuels nodded mutely.

All at once the Doctor spotted Wilkins and pointed at him. 'I know you, don't I? Wilkins, isn't it?'

'Yes, sir,' said Wilkins in a weak voice, instinctively standing to attention.

'At ease, soldier,' said the Doctor casually. He strolled across to the bed, peering into Major Daker's ruddy face.

'And I'm guessing you must be Major Daker?' he said. 'I met your horse, briefly.' Before Daker could even contemplate how to respond to that, the Doctor asked, 'How are you feeling now, Major?'

'I've… never been better,' Daker spluttered.

'Glad to hear it,' said the Doctor, sounding as if he genuinely was. 'Have you back on the parade ground, terrorising the troops, in no time, eh?' Again, before Daker had chance to reply, he continued, 'Actually you're just the sort of reliable, no-nonsense, efficient feller I'm looking for. Tell me, Major Daker, how quickly do you reckon you'll be able to organise a major rescue operation?'

Donna opened her eyes and concentrated on trying not to be sick. On all sides of her people were staggering about, looking around in disbelief. Some screamed or burst into tears, unable to cope with the sheer impossibility of instantaneous travel.

Adelaide appeared at her shoulder, looking pale. 'Am I dreaming?' she said faintly. 'Or are we really outside?'

Donna looked at the pink and purple sky, beneath which the hills loomed black and forbidding. People were streaming from the cave openings like ants from a disturbed nest, many not even stopping when they were out, but simply running down the rocky slope as if demons were after them. It would be impossible even for the Doctor, Donna thought, to round all these people up and take them home. She wondered what would become of them, and consoled herself with the thought that at least a long walk back to Calcutta was better than a lonely, terrifying death on a planet millions of miles away.

'Yeah,' she said. 'Yeah, we're outside.'

Adelaide looked at the disc in Donna's hand with an expression of awe. 'What *is* that device?'

Before Donna could answer, Sir Edgar appeared, his wife in tow.

'I say,' he said, 'where the devil are we?'

Donna shook her head. 'I've no idea.'

'But how do you propose we get back to Calcutta?' Mary demanded querulously.

Donna scowled. 'I dunno, do I? Walk, I suppose.'

'*Walk?*' squawked Mary. 'It could be miles. And it's getting dark. There might be snakes. Perhaps even robbers.'

Donna's temper suddenly flared. 'Yeah, well, if they had any sense they'd run a mile if they saw you coming. I mean, what do you *honestly* expect me to do, lady? Call a cab? Give you a piggyback? Wave a magic wand?'

Mary looked as if she had stepped into a sudden gale-force wind.

'I hardly— ' Sir Edgar began, but his voice was drowned out by the familiar trumpeting grind of ancient engines.

Donna whirled round, grinning, as the TARDIS materialised. The door opened and the Doctor stuck his head out.

'Anyone need a lift?' he said.

FOURTEEN

'This vehicle terminates here,' the Doctor announced. 'Will all passengers please disembark.'

They had already dropped the Campbells off at home. Now they were about to deliver Gandhi, Gopal, Ranjit and Edward Morgan back to the camp.

For the few minutes duration of the short double-trip, the TARDIS had been busier than Donna had ever seen it.

The Doctor had spent the journey circling the TARDIS console, checking readings and adjusting things and generally being a bit aloof from all the astonished goggling and incredulous chatter going on below. Donna suspected that the Doctor didn't like having so many people in the TARDIS, even if it *was* just for a few minutes. She knew that once a job was over he generally preferred to slip quietly away, to move on with as little fuss as possible.

When the Campbells had departed moments earlier, he hadn't got involved in all the hugs and handshakes and goodbyes, but had remained standing at the console, from where he had simply stuck up a hand and shouted a cheery, 'See ya.'

Now they had materialised at the camp, and Donna wondered whether his goodbyes here would be just as perfunctory.

However, as soon as he pulled the lever to open the doors he leaped down from the console platform and, tilting his head at Donna as an indication that she should join him, followed his passengers outside.

The TARDIS had landed between two of the medical tents, out of sight of the majority of refugees. The group from the TARDIS looked out across the camp, which, despite the devastation caused by the gelem warriors, was already returning to normal. With nowhere else to go, the homeless of Calcutta were slowly filtering back to their makeshift shelters. Everywhere Donna looked, she saw repairs being made to the flimsy dwellings, fires being lit against the chill of the night.

Two small children spotted Gandhi and their eyes widened in wonder. When one of them murmured, 'Bapu,' Gandhi gave them one of his familiar, near-toothless grins and ambled across to talk to them.

'Just want to double-check something,' the Doctor

muttered to Donna and followed Edward and Gopal into the nearest medical tent. Instantly the few staff that had remained behind and had managed to evade the clutches of the gelem warriors crowded around them.

'It's a miracle, Dr Morgan!' one of the staff said excitedly.

'They are cured! They are all cured!' exclaimed another.

Edward held up his hands, looking flustered. 'Please,' he said, 'one at a time. Will someone kindly explain what you're talking about.'

The half-dozen auxiliaries looked at one another, and as if at some unspoken agreement a young, bespectacled Indian man stepped forward.

'The patients in the isolation tent, Dr Morgan,' he said, trying to contain his excitement, 'they are all better. Even the most advanced cases are no longer displaying any symptoms of their illness.'

Edward looked stunned. 'But... that's impossible,' he spluttered.

'Nah,' said the Doctor, 'that's energy inversion. I rigged the Jal Karath ship so that it would hoover up and neutralise every zytron particle within a thousand mile radius when it imploded.'

He looked round at the crescent of blank faces regarding him, and sighed. 'Look, all you need to know is that I did something incredibly clever and now everyone's better.' Abruptly he clapped his hands. 'Right, back to work. There are still plenty of sick and hungry people out there, you know.'

As everyone got back to work, the Doctor looked at Donna and jerked his head towards the exit flap, indicating that they should leave.

Outside the tent they found Gandhi sitting cross-legged on the ground, still talking quietly to the children. As the Doctor and Donna approached, the little man jumped nimbly to his feet.

'Right, Mohandas, we're off,' the Doctor said briskly. He held out a hand, and then, thinking better of it, abruptly stepped forward and embraced the little man. 'It's been a pleasure and a privilege,' he murmured before stepping back, uncharacteristically lost for words.

Gandhi beamed. 'And for me too, Doctor,' he said. 'Where will you go now?'

'Oh, you know,' said the Doctor vaguely, 'other times and places.'

'See you, Mohandas,' Donna said. She leaned forward to kiss his cheek. 'You look after yourself.'

Gandhi winked at the children, who were watching the exchange with interest. 'You see,' he said drily, 'even at my advanced age I have not lost my touch with the ladies.'

'You old rascal,' Donna said as the children giggled. 'Goodbye. And good luck with… everything.'

She and the Doctor walked across to the TARDIS, stopping at the door to wave one last time before going inside.

As the Doctor busied himself at the console, Donna looked at the image of the little man on the scanner screen.

'What happens to him?' she asked.

The Doctor looked at her for a moment, sadness on his face. Softly he said, 'On 30 January next year, he'll be assassinated. Someone will step out of a crowd of well-wishers and shoot him in the heart.'

Donna put a hand to her mouth. Tears sparkled in her eyes. In a wavering voice she said, 'Who would do that? Why would anyone want to kill someone like him?'

The Doctor shrugged. 'There's always someone who doesn't agree with what you're trying to do,' he said simply.

Donna continued to stare at the serene face of the little man on the screen, too upset to speak.

The Doctor sidled up and slipped an arm around her shoulders. In a quiet voice he said, 'His last words as he lay on the ground were "Hey Rama", which means "Oh God". Witnesses say that as he died his face wore a serene smile and his body was surrounded by a halo of divine light.'

Donna sniffed. Still tearful, she said, 'He reminds me a lot of you, you know.'

The Doctor's face was sombre. He reached out and pulled the lever that would propel the TARDIS into the Time Vortex.

'Oh, he's far more forgiving than I'll ever be,' he said.

Acknowledgements

Thanks to Justin, Steve, Gary, Mark, Simon, David and Catherine, for oiling the wheels. And special thanks to my children, David and Polly, for being my encouraging and enthusiastic target audience.

DOCTOR·WHO

The Many Hands
by Dale Smith
ISBN 978 1 84607 422 6
UK £6.99 US $11.99/$14.99 CDN

The Nor' Loch is being filled in. If you ask the soldiers
there, they'll tell you it's a stinking cesspool that the
city can do without. But that doesn't explain why the
workers won't go near the place without an armed
guard.

That doesn't explain why they whisper stories about
the loch giving up its dead, about the minister who
walked into his church twelve years after he died…

It doesn't explain why, as they work, they whisper
about a man called the Doctor.

And about the many hands of Alexander Monro.

DOCTOR·WHO

Starships and Spacestations

by Justin Richards

ISBN 978 1 84607 423 3

£7.99 US $12.99/$15.99 CDN

The Doctor has his TARDIS to get him from place to place and time to time, but the rest of the Universe relies on more conventional transport… From the British Space Programme of the late twentieth century to Earth's Empire in the far future, from the terrifying Dalek Fleet to deadly Cyber Ships, this book documents the many starships and spacestations that the Doctor and his companions have encountered on their travels.

He has been held prisoner in space, escaped from the moon, witnessed the arrival of the Sycorax and the crash landing of a space pig… More than anyone else, the Doctor has seen the development of space travel between countless worlds.

This stunningly illustrated book tells the amazing story of Earth's ventures into space, examines the many alien fleets who have paid Earth a visit, and explores the other starships and spacestations that the Doctor has encountered on his many travels…

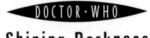